BLOOD PASSION

BOOK III

CHILD OF MALICE

J.M. VALENTE

Cover Design by J.M.Valente

Blood Passion Book III

Child Of Malice

Cover Design by J.M.Valente

Library of Congress Control Number: 2018938689

ISBN-13: Paperback: 978-1-64151-659-4

Hardback: 978-1-64398-964-8

....

First Printing

....

....

....

Printed in the United States of America

LitFire LLC

1-800-511-9787

www.litfirepublishing.com

order@litfirepublishing.com

Contents

Praise for
BLOOD PASSION-BOOK III
~CHILD OF MALICE

"J.M. Valente's BLOOD PASSION-Book III~Child Of Malice is a highly intense, white-knuckled ride that is guaranteed to captivate your interest, and satiate your fancy for the macabre from the opening page right through to the jaw dropping astonishing bonus Prequel Novella at the end. Once again, a love/hate relationship is masterfully cultivated by Valente for the reader in Rachael Valli, a Human Hybrid Living Vampire, who has now come of age with ferocity. "Child Of Malice" is an engrossing, fascinating, and, yes, addictive novel that I found hard to put down. Definitely a must read, especially for the Modern Gothic Horror genre lovers."

Jeannie Flynn

~Acknowledgments~

A special appreciation to
my Beta reader, Jeannie Flynn.

~~~~~~~~~~~~~~~~~~~~

Also for help with the editing;
my GINGER Editing Program
&
My KINDLE FIRE
and to Alexa,
my Amazon ECHO & DOT
~~~~~~~~~~~~~~~~~~~~

~Dedication~

To my Sons:
James II & Vincent,
And to their Mother:
My late X-Wife, Mary Beth D'Amore.
(1951~2015)

Other BLOOD PASSION Novels
By J.M.VALENTE

~~~~~~~~~~~~~~~~~~~~~~~~~~~~~~~~~~~~~

BLOOD PASSION
~BOOK I~

BLOOD PASSION
~BOOK II~
FAMILY BLOOD
~~~~~~~~~~~~~~~~~~~~~~~~~~~~~~~~~~~~~

Chapter One

RACHAEL SITS AT the Desk in the Library office, in her sleeping attire and robe, finishes her third reading of the Memoirs of her real Father; Michael Valli. She sits back in her chair to think about changing her Surname from DeClerico to Valli, wondering if her Mother would mind or be upset with her, if she did this.

Her train of thought is interrupted by the sound of the front door bell ringing:

Now, who could this be? I'm not expecting anyone to come by this early in the morning. Well, there's only one way to find out, who's at my door, and that is to answer it.

So, with a slight grumble, she opens the middle drawer of the Desk puts the Memoir in, closes and locks it, rises from her chair, places the drawer key on the small lip above the Library archway framework, then leans out of the archway looks to her left to see in the large decorative cut glass oval centre of the inner door, that it's Lucy and Bobby standing in the foyer. Lucy looks in and sees her, waves, and calls out loudly,

"Rach, it's me and Bobby!"

She walks to the inner door and opens it, saying

"I can see that. Silly! Come in, give me a minute to get dressed, I'll be right down."

So as Rachael makes her way quickly up the Grand Staircase.

Bobby scoldingly declares to Lucy,

"I told ya we should'a called first!"

"Yeah yeah!"

Lucy snidely replies, as she looks around and continues, "I still can't believe she's living in this big house all by herself."

Bobby proclaims, as he peeks into the Library,

"Lucy, this place gives me the creeps!"

"Yeah, me too, a little!"

Bobby continues, "I still can't believe that she actually owns it out right!"

Rachael reappears at the bottom of the Grand Staircase in her jeans and T-shirt and proclaims,

"Well, Bobby, I do, I have the clear title to prove it. Do you want to see it?"

"No Rach, I believe that you do, it's just so… so… big for just one person to be living in!"

"So people, what's up? What brings you guys to my humble abode so early this morning?" Rachael asks of them both, changing the subject.

"Lucy has an idea that she just couldn't wait to talk to you about!" Bobby informs her.

"Okay, guys, let's go to the Kitchen and we can sit and talk in there. I could use some grape juice. I also have orange or tomato juice, if you don't want grape!"

"I'll have orange," Bobby requests.

"Tomato, for me." Lucy answers.

As Rachael serves them their juice, she requests of them.

"So like I said, or should say, inquired. What brings you two here this morning?"

Lucy fields the question, answering,

"Well, Rach, you've owned this place. What? About two months now, and you've been living here for about a month, you really need to have a house warming party, don't you think?"

Bobby enthusiastically chimes in,

"Yeah, a really big, hot house warming party!"

"Rach, I'm going to try to get myself a job at the Mystic Pizza," Lucy states and asks, "What about you?"

"Lucy, with the money that I have inherited from my late Great Grandfather, Romeo from my Grandmother Carmella I have plenty."

And she adds to herself,

Plus all the money that was hidden in the old chest under the Grand Staircase, that only I now know about.

I really don't need to get a job."

They both look at her with envious eyes and simultaneously ask,

"Then what do you plan on doing with yourself?"

"I'm not sure yet, haven't made up my mind, between writing a book, or becoming a model! Maybe I'll go for both?" she answers them flamboyantly, and continues, "It's not uncommon for a Girl of my age to become an author or a model."

Lucy interjects,

"Yeah, I know, an author like that teenage Girl that wrote... what was it? Twinkle, or something like that... ah, oh darn... what was her name?

Rachael interrupts with,

"Oh, Lucy, what her name is doesn't matter, you both know of whom I'm talking about, if she can do it, so can I! I already have some good subject matter for an interesting story."

Rachael suddenly has a quick thought,

A story similar to my real Father and my Mom's might be good, just have'ta change the names and location is all, and make it a bit more romantic.

"Yeah yeah, that all sounds really cool, but what about the party?"

Bobby interrupts the flow of the conversation excitedly, and continues, "I could get a lot of the freshmen, sophomores and maybe some of the seniors from my fraternity to come and some of the Girls on campus as well! I could post it on the bulletin board in the campus Library. We can make it like, the event of the season!"

"Okay, alright, but we'll need some time for the planning of it!" Rachael instructs and continues, "How about in three weeks, that should be enough time to get a caterer and a D.J. lined up, and if the weather's good it can be in the Backyard, right?" She continues, "Lucy, when you go to the Mystic Pizza, to see about getting yourself a job, you can also ask them about them doing the catering for the party."

Bobby abruptly chimes in,

"That sounds awesome. In about three weeks, my buddy, Shane, who's a D.J. with 'MusicSmith' which he co-owns with his cousin, that recently did the music for our frat house party, is coming in from New York City this week to do a party near by and hang for a while; I can probably get **him** to do the music for the party!"

Lucy enthusiastically stands up, claps her hands together and proclaims,

"Okay then, it's all settled, we'll make this the event to remember!"

With that settled, they say their goodbyes, and take their leave of the Cliff House, and convey that they'll be in touch.

As they walk down the front stairs to where Bobby's Car is parked on the street, Rachael can hear Bobby say to Lucy,

"This is gonna be **the** party of the year!"

"Oh, yeah, It's gonna be so, **fab**!" Lucy agrees.

Rachael closes the door, turns on her heels and with a deep sigh, goes back to the Library to turn on her Laptop and open the word processor program. And get back out her Father's Memoirs to make a start on writing her Manuscript for a novel, just like her Father had intended to write a book, before his strange clandestine encounter up in the Attic of this very house, which changed his life and his mind to writing his Memoirs.

As she begins to plan how and where her novel will begin thinking;

*The writing of my Father's Memoir is rather detailed and focused on his dealing and living with, what he refers to as the **Blood Passion**, and having two different personalities, somewhat like the summer reading book I had in*

between tenth and eleventh grade: ***The Strange Case of Dr. Jekyll and Mr. Hyde*** by ***Robert Louis Stevenson.***

My Dad goes on about how he felt about ending people's existence in order for him to survive, and how his animal aspect really had no trouble with it, but his Human attribute had to deal with the guilt. Strangely, he would mentally communicate with this persona he named ***Malice Nightwing****, his animal characteristic. I, although have inherited his thirst and need for ingesting Blood of a living being. Thank heaven; I don't have the dual personalities like my Dad, and my Godmother Marlena, most likely had, because she had become a Vampire in the same way he did.*

That makes me a somewhat different type of, for the lack of a better name, Vampire, and on the subject of strange things how did the Bat get Mutated and get here in the Attic; two questions, I'll probably never know the answer to. Where he had difficulty in the control of this ***Blood Passion*** *at first, I have had up till now plenty of control of my Blood feastings, but I have not indulged in the taking of Human Blood, hence the ending of a Human life. What would that be like? I wonder and how will I deal with it, will it change me in any way? Once I indulge in the taking of Human Blood? Will I then need it for my survival like it was for my Father and Marlena? My indulging of the occasional animal Blood feast is like ingesting a super strong vitamin almost like* Roids. *So many questions; I suppose, the answers may come in time. But the desire to indulge in Human Blood, this* ***Blood Passion*** *so to speak is beginning, to get stronger as I get older; I can feel it, stimulating inside me. Well, it's all in my Dad's Memoirs, of how to go about living with it, like a manual of sorts. I suppose I should thank my Father for writing this, It should and will be very helpful to me.*

Rachael sits back in her chair and states with affection out loud,

"Thank you, Dear Father, for writing your Memoirs, I do so hope that you can hear me somehow, wherever you might be, because I do believe that you… I mean your essence is not in the house anymore. Because of my lack of contact with your ethereal spirit, so you must have moved on. May you now, rest in peace, and take my Love with you, I pray, Dear Father. I must now deal with my life on my own, just as you had to deal with yours."

She leans forward in her chair to place her fingers on her Laptop keyboard, and says softly,

"Okay now… opening line… let me see. Ah yes."

And begins to type;

The night was sultry; the light of the full moon brilliantly, illuminates the slightly damp pavement in the street. It is a Bella Luna night.

Is what according to her Father's Memoirs, her Great-Grandfather Romeo, would have endowed it to be!

With that memorable thought done, continues on with the typing of her Manuscript;

Mia, in her late twenties is a lovely young Woman of five feet two inches, with long dark brown hair, and a voluptuous figure, tries desperately to shrink into the passenger seat of Marcus's Black Sports Car and disappear into it. She hadn't realized how much of her loyalty had been tied to having him; this six foot tall Man, with light brown hair, hazel eyes, and an above average body of a man in his early thirties, in her life.

It has only been slightly two weeks that Mia and Marcus have known each other, but in this short amount of time he has changed her outlook on life. Without him, she knows in her heart of hearts, that all of the resurrected confidence he has stimulated in her would disappear and expire.

Chapter Two

RACHAEL IS SLIGHTLY startled, which interrupts her from her writing by her Cell-phone vibrating on the Desk; she looks at it to see that it's her Mother calling. She answers it questioningly,

"Hi Mother, What's up?"

"Hello sweetheart, are you all settled into the Cliff House, we miss you already."

"Oh, Mom, really, I've only been gone for a month, how is my little Brother Mathew, I suppose he misses me also?"

"Yes, he does and so does your Stepfather, Joseph. So we want you to be here for dinner on Sunday. Please say that you will come!"

"Yes, okay, I will come to dinner on Sunday, Mom; there are some things I need to discuss with you!"

"Such as?"

Mina answers her inquisitively.

"We'll talk, on Sunday."

She responds to her, being vague.

"Okay then, we'll see you about two on Sunday!"

Mina happily replies.

"Yes, Mom, I need to hang up now, my Love to you, Mathew and Joseph, bye."

Mina returns the sentiments and reluctantly hangs up.

Rachael believes this will be a good time and opportunity to talk to her Mother about changing her, Sir Name and discuss with her about obtaining Marlena's Car that's been in the garage, ever since Marlena's strange disappearance, to everyone, except her and her Mother, and also find out about buying it for herself.

She continues on about the Car with the thought;

I will definitely have to have the color changed from red to black, it will obviously look so fetch, in black with the red interior.

She then closes her Laptop Computer, and makes her way to the Kitchen to make some Coffee to have with her Breakfast.

With her Coffee in hand, and a small bowl of cereal goes out the back door and sits in the Gazebo to enjoy the lovely sunny morning, while eating, looks around in the Backyard and the tree with the one word **'Nightwing'** carved into it, and after reading her Father's Memoir, Rachael now knows that; herself, her Mother, and probably Marlena before her demise, had read them, making them the only people that know, precisely what it represents. As she sits in front of her empty bowl, and now the cold half cup of Coffee, she spies a good size raccoon run across the yard and fights off the urge to go after it for a Blood feast.

She ponders on an idea of what she might do to get rid of the carving in the tree, she can't think of anything that would work to get rid of it or cover it up, and doing so may make it even more obvious to the casual observer. Besides, it's somewhat of a memento of her real Father, and if asked about it she'll just simply explain it away, as a young imaginative person's tree art.

It being Saturday night, she would usually meet up with her friends at the Mystic Pizza Restaurant, and make a night of it, but for some unknown reason she's not up for it tonight. So, she'll do a bit of lite reading and make an early night of it, for she has a lot to discuss with her Mother tomorrow after their Sunday dinner.

Rachael rises about ten on Sunday morning, has a light Breakfast of fruit and yogurt. Goes up to her Bedroom to pick out an outfit to wear to dinner at her Mother's. She remembers a dress that her Mother had bought her for her last Birthday when she turned twenty, which she has not worn yet, and decides to wear it.

Rachael arrives at where she grew up, at ninety nine Elm Place about one in the afternoon. Her little Brother Mathew hears her scooter pull into the driveway and runs out to greet her with an affectionate hug proclaiming,

"Hello Sis, don't you look all the beautiful young Woman in that pretty dress."

Rachael replies,

"Why, thank you, Bro, and don't you look the grown up young Man in your Sunday suit."

"Yeah, we went to a late morning Mass and Mom wanted me to stay in it to show you."

"I'm glad she did, because you look super in it!"

At that moment, Mina shows up at the door and calls them in, since she's about to put out, the salad on the table."

They both acknowledge her simultaneously with,

"Be right in, Mom!"

After a delicious dinner, Joseph sits in his easy chair to read his Sunday Newspaper, Mathew runs up to his room to change out of his Sunday suit and into his play clothes. As Mina loads the Dishwasher, Rachael approaches her and requests anxiously,

"Mom, could I have your undivided attention, please, there's a couple of things I'd like to discuss with you."

"Sure, sweetheart, just let me get your Stepfather a fresh cup of Coffee, and then you'll have my attention."

Rachael sits at the Kitchen table and patiently waits for her Mother to be finished with her things, as Mathew comes running into the Kitchen with his Baseball bat and glove to announce, that he's off to the park to play with his friends.

Mina acknowledges him, and then sits at the table and says,

"Okay, Dear, I'm all yours. What is it you needed to talk to me about?"

Rachael lowers her head and begins,

"Okay Mom, you're probably not going to like what I have to ask you, but here goes."

She raises her head, looks her Mother right in her eyes and begins,

"I've known for a while now, the my real Father's last name is Valli, so I would like to..."

Mina cuts her off with,

"And I suppose you want to change your name to Valli?"

"You really don't need to ask me for permission to do so; you're almost twenty one you can do it then, whatever I may say."

"I know that Mom, I just wanted to pass it by you first, to see how you felt about it, you don't think Joseph will be hurt by me doing it, would you, and please don't tell me to ask him, as it is hard enough for me to approach you with it."

"Well, sweetheart, Joseph knows the truth, he has known it since before you were born, so I believe he'd give you his blessings to claim your birthright," Mina states and continues, "So I'd think you researched it and know how to go about it. Right?

"Yes, Mom, I have, but because I'm not twenty-one yet, I'll be needing you to sign off on it, please."

"Yes, of course I will, if it would make you happy, sweetheart! Just bring me the papers to sign when you get them"

"To be honest with you Mom, I've already acquired them on-line and printed them out, I have them with me in the compartment under the seat of the scooter. And speaking of the scooter that's the next thing I want to talk to you about!"

"Is there something wrong with it Dear, because you can take it to my Mechanic, I'm sure he'd fix it for you."

"No, Mom, there's nothing wrong with it, I'm just getting a little too old to be driving around with it, I wanted to move up to a Car."

"Oh, I see, and what do you have in mind about that?"

"I would like to buy Marlena's little M.G. Automobile that's been sitting in my garage for some time now, that's what I have in mind about that, Dear sweet Mother. So what do you think?"

"Well, I'd say you will need to talk to her Sister Madeline about that!"

"That's what I thought, but I wasn't sure, so I'll need to get her number from you."

"Sure, but do you want me, to ask her about it?"

"No, Mom, I should be the one to handle this."

"Okay, here's her number!"

"By the way Mom, I'm having a house warming party soon, wasn't really my idea, it was Lucy's, I would like you guys to come, I'll give you the particulars as soon as I know them."

"Well, yes, Dear, we will come, but we wouldn't stay long."

"Yes, that's fine, as long as you guys come for a little while. Okay then I'll be in touch!"

Rachael pokes her head into the Living Room to say goodbye to Joseph, and turns around to kiss Mina good bye saying,

"Dinner was awesome as usual, Mom, talk to you soon."

And after giving Mina the change of Sir Name paperwork for her to sign, she takes her leave, with the signed document.

Chapter Three

RACHAEL ARIVES BACK to the Cliff House, to find Lucy and Bobby sitting on the front steps. She pulls up the driveway, and into the garage, where there's just enough room to get the Scooter in beside Marlena's M.G. Sports Car.

Lucy runs up the driveway somewhat excited to find out about what happened between Rachael and her Mother.

Slightly out of breath, she asks,

"So, Rach, how did it go with your Mother?"

Rachael replies,

"Good, she agreed to the name change," And as she gestures to the M.G. Car and continues, "and me buying this Car from Marlena's Sister, she gave me Madeline's phone number, I'll call her tomorrow."

Lucy continues with her questioning, asking inquisitively,

"So, when you buy the Car, what will you do with the Scooter?"

"Well, I'm not sure yet," she replies slyly, "Lucy, you do have a Birthday coming soon, don't you?"

"Yeah, it will be my twenty first next month!"

"I can't, for the life of me, imagine what you might, what me to give you," Rachael replies deviously.

Lucy then lowers her head, after purposely putting her hand on the Scooter and says,

"I'm sure you'll think of something, Bit-chin."

The rest of their conversation is interrupted by Bobby approaching and asking,

"Lucy, did you tell Rach what you found out about the catering of the party by the Mystic Pizza?"

"I was just about to when you showed up!"

So, Bobby announces,

"Well, don't let me, stop you!"

Rachael stops them both by requesting,

"Let's continue this inside," as she begins to walk in the direction of the back door saying, "Come on, I could use a soda and you guys might like one too?

They both nod in agreement and follow her in the back door.

As they sit around the Kitchen table, enjoying their sodas,

Rachael inquires of Lucy,

"So Lucy, what happened at the Mystic Pizza?"

Lucy perks up and answers with,

"Yeah, well, I filled out an application for a job, and then talked with Jojo about the catering for the party."

"And she said what?"

Rachael inquires impatiently.

"I've a good chance of getting a job there…"

Bobby looks up from his smart phone and chimes in a little agitated,

"Lucy, we want to know about the catering!"

Rachael takes Lucy's hand, and interjects with,

"Lucy, that's really great about you getting a job there, but what we actually need to know is about the catering, so please tell us what Jojo said about it."

"Yeah, Okay, she said that they need at least two weeks notice, they have a mobile Pizza oven van that they park on site for up to four hours. Their four hour plan is about four hundred dollars, which gets you unlimited Pizza and soda; they do have shorter time plans for less money."

"That's great Lucy, you did good! So guys how about we do it the weekend after next, Bobby would that give you enough time to put the notices up?"

"Sounds rad, more than enough, I'll put them up on Tuesday!"

"Okay, then guys, I guess we have that in the bag, and we can talk more about it during the week to get what else we'll need."

"Lucy we better get going now, I need to get to my dorm, and get started on the notices."

Bobby states.

As they make their way out to Bobby's Car parked out front. Bobby ads,

"I'll call Shane for the music, Rach; you'd better call the Mystic Pizza by tomorrow."

"Will do, talk with you guys soon, drive save Bobby!"

"Don't I always!"

Monday morning comes to Rachael at about ten. As she sits in the Kitchen having her usual light Breakfast, she reaches back to the pocket in her jacket hanging on the door knob of the back door, and pulls out the piece of paper with Madeline's number on it, finishes her meal and dials the number. After three rings, someone with a Man's voice answers,

"Hello?"

She replies,

"Hello, is Madeline Decenti there, please?"

"Hold on a moment, may I say who's calling?"

"Yes, it's Rachael Val… DeClerico."

"Hello, Rachael, what may I do for you?"

"Well, your Sister's Car is still here at the Cliff House, and I was wondering if you might sell it to me."

"Oh, yes the Car, I almost forgot about it, and with you being her Godchild, I would like you, to have it, shall we say, as a late graduation gift. I'll draw up a bill of sale, and get out the title, and send them to you right away."

"Oh my God! Thank you so much, that's so generous of you!"

"Think nothing of it Dear, I'm pretty sure that's what my Sister would have wanted."

"Okay then I'll say goodbye and thanks again!"

"Yes, my Dear, goodbye."

Rachael then, contacts the Mystic Pizza Restaurant and makes the reservation with Jojo, for the catering of the party. Then goes into the Library, and does a little more writing on her Manuscript, after writing a little, she takes a break, to make a call to her Mother, and leaves a message on her phone about the date for the party, and also calls and leaves a message with her Me-Ma and Granddad for them to come.

She then goes back to the writing of her Manuscript, and by the time it is close to three in the afternoon, she is interrupted by her Doorbell ringing.

She thinks;

Now who can this be at my door? There is only one best way to find out.

She comes out of the Library to see, through the glass window of the inside door of the foyer, a young Man standing at the outside door. She holds down the button on the intercom and asks,

"Hello, what can I do for you?"

An answer comes in a somewhat familiar voice.

As he tries to look in to see, who it is that he's conversing with he asks,

"Rachael, is that you?"

"Excuse me, do I know **you**? You certainly seem to know, **me**!"

"Rachael, Rachael DeClerico, it's me James, I mean, well, you'd remember me as, Jimmy Varlino!"

"Oh my God!" she exclaims, as she buzzes the outside door to let him in, and then opens the inside door, she continues, "Please come in, it's been a long time!"

Chapter Four

RACHAEL OPENS THE door wide to let James in, as he passes her, she looks out at the street, to notice there's no Vehicle parked in front, or at the beginning of the driveway of the Cliff House. James turns around slowly to look at the décor, and proclaims,

"Rachael, I understand you own this house now. May I ask how that came to be?"

"Well, James, that's kind of a long, sordid story, why don't we go into the Kitchen, I was just going to make a pot of Coffee."

"Thanks, I'd Love some."

As they make their way to the Kitchen, Rachael has a thought,

I'm going to have to make a cover story; the truth would be too harsh and unbelievable.

As James waits the twenty minutes for the Coffee to brew, he takes a walk out in the Backyard and sits in one of the swings of the swing set. As soon as the Coffee is done, Rachael calls him into the Kitchen from the back door.

As Rachael pours and serves the Coffee, James declares,

"You haven't changed much of anything; I saw a few personal touches, but nothing major, you even kept the swing set."

"Well, James, your Mom did such a wonderful job of decorating this house; I didn't find much I wanted, or needed to change, and why wouldn't I keep the swing set!"

"By the way, James may I ask how you got here, and why? With that asked, she continues, "I didn't notice a Vehicle parked out front or in the driveway."

"Oh Yeah, sure, I'm on my way to Providence, Rhode Island by, Amtrak train, and planned to make a stop in Mystic, and visit a few friends I hadn't seen in a while. Walking down Main Street, I ran into one of them, from when my family and I lived here at the Cliff House, before my Father disappeared, and then arrangements were made for my Sister Gabrielle and me, to stay, and live with my Aunt Madeline, and Uncle Frank in Hartford, after spending a weekend with them. He told me that you own it and lived here now, so I took it upon myself to check out what he told me, and get a chance to see you again, you probably don't or never knew it, but I always had a thing for you when we were younger."

"Now that **is** something I didn't know, you never really gave me any clue that you felt that way about me!"

"Well, Rachael, me and about a dozen other guys in Mystic had a thing for you," He lowers his head and continues, "Back then as a young Girl, you were the Bomb, as we Boys would say about a gorgeous Girl, which is what we all thought you were, and I can see even more so, that you are still, as a young Woman."

"Thank you, James, I'm totally flattered, and James, I was then, and still am, so sorry about what happened to your Sister, Gabrielle."

"Yeah, that really sucked, she was so young, and her life was just beginning."

"Yes, it was. She was a beautiful Girl, and I'm sure she would have been an even more beautiful Woman. Life can really suck like that."

"Okay, so much for reminiscing, so how did you, come to own the Cliff House?"

Rachael stops to collect her thoughts and thinks,

He would have to get back to that, I thought if we started talking about our younger days, he'd forget he asked, and drop it, so now I'll need to come up with something to tell him that won't sound too, lame. But first, I'll need to stall for a little time,

"James before I get into that, how much time before your next train leaves?"

"Ah, let me see," He claims, stands up to pull out the train schedule from his back pocket, checks it and continues,

"The next train is due in about five hours."

"Well, are you hungry? Because we can get a delivery from the Ebb Tide Restaurant, for us, I'm feeling a little peckish myself, and could use a bite. I do have their delivery menu right on the counter here," she then stands up to get it, turns around and hands it to him, saying,

"Here have a look and see if anything takes your fancy. And it's on me, a little reunion meal so to speak. Once you decide what you would like to eat, and call to give them our order, you can go down to the Wine Cellar and get us a bottle of Wine, I do believe there is some bottles left, that was sent over from your Mothers' family Vineyard in France, that your Aunt didn't take when she cleared the place for selling. When you decide what it is that you want. You can order me, a Sirloin Steak dinner, rare, with a baked potato, and any vegetable that comes with it, and if you don't want Wine with your meal, you'll find sodas in the Fridge, I, myself would Love a bottle of Wine with my Steak. In the meantime, I'd like to go upstairs to freshen up, a bit."

James nods in agreement.

Rachael makes her way up the Grand Staircase, as she reaches to the top, and turns in the direction of the Bathroom, her head starts to pound intensely, she puts out her hand to brace herself against the wall, so as to keep from falling down. She takes a deep breath and her head stops pounding. She gets to the Bathroom, and looks in the mirror, at her face to notice, to her horror, that her eyes have turned from hazel to red. She quickly closes them for a few seconds, and when she opens them, they are back to looking normal. She breathes a deep sigh of relief, washes her face and hands. Goes to her room to change into a fresh blouse, as she's buttoning up, she has a hot flash, and then an intensely deep cold feeling takes her to her knees. She stays there for a few seconds, hoping it will pass as quickly as it came.

As she pauses, in her kneeling position, she remembers that in her Father's Memoirs, about his transformations from his own persona to having Malice take over, for their Blood feedings, he noted about his eye color going from hazel to red, signaling a time for a feeding on Human Blood. She cups her face in her hands and thinks,

*Oh Dear Lord, could this be the time for my hunger for Human Blood to be initializing? If that's the case I should get James out of the house, but then what would I do for a feeding on Human Blood, I may need this to survive, so either **he** dies, or I **do**.*

At this time, she begins to feel the Blood within her veins, heat up, and her head starts pounding again. She gives it a few more moments, and these strange effects quickly subside. Somewhat unsteady on her feet, she lifts herself to a standing position, with the help of the vanity chair. With her best effort, she composes herself and makes her way to the top of the Grand Staircase.

She takes in a deep breath, and with one hand on the banister starts her slow descend, of both the stairs, and what she now believes could, and must be, her first steps in finally becoming, a fully fledged living Vampire, like her real Father; Michael Valli, and her Godmother; Marlena Varlino, were before her.

As she enters the Kitchen, she inquires of James,

"So, I take it, that the food is on its way."

"Yeah, they told me it should arrive in about an hour, and I decided to have the chicken ala Ebb Tide. You must order from them quite a lot, because when I gave them the address, they just said okay, and told me that it would be here straightaway."

"Yes, both my Mother and I have ordered from them often, their food is superb, and their delivery service is also first-rate, and I will say you made a great choice for yourself, and I see you brought up a bottle of Wine, thank you. Okay then, let's set up out back in the Gazebo, it really is a pleasant place for having a meal, in the late afternoon."

Chapter Five

WHILE JAMES BRINGS the utensils, napkins and condiments out to the Gazebo, Rachael sits at the Kitchen table thinking about what just happened to her upstairs;

*It was strange for my eyes to change color on their own like that, I normally have control over my transformations when I'm in need of a Blood feast, these new effects I'm feeling must be the signs of my next steps in the metamorphosis of my Vampirism. Will I be going from a Blood feast, which is of animal Blood, to the **Blood Passion** for Human Blood?*

These thoughts of hers' are interrupted by James entering the Kitchen and asking,

"Rach, is there anything else we will need for our dinner?"

Rachael doesn't answer him right away.

James leans in close beside her and repeats his question. She then abruptly comes out of her thoughts and answers him with,

"Oh, James, ah yes sorry, you can bring out two Wine glasses, if you will be having some Wine with your dinner, I certainly will be with mine."

"Yes, I do believe I will be having some Wine also."

"Good, they should be here soon with our meal; you can open the Wine to let it breathe."

James opens the Wine, and sits down next to her, and asks once again,

"So, Rach, are you going to tell me how you came to own the Cliff House?"

"Why yes, but let's enjoy our dinner first, and then I'll tell you how it came, to me owning this place. By the way, James, have you decided on an occupation yet, if I remember correctly, you were always saying how you wanted to be an athlete of some sort. Right?"

"Yeah, Rach, I wanted that when I was a young Boy, but now I'm thinking more on the lines of becoming a lawyer like my Dad was."

"Wow, that sounds super, isn't that a lot of schooling though?"

"Yeah, but I do have all of my Father's law books, which will save me quite a bit of money."

"Cool, I'd like to wish you good luck with it, and maybe my Dad… Joseph could be of some help to you with that."

"Oh, I was thinking of stopping back here in Mystic on my return trip to Hartford, to meet and talk to him about it."

"I'm sure he'd do whatever he could to help you, after all he and your Dad collaborated on a few cases from time to time."

"Yeah, that's right; I do remember them doing that."

"All right then James, while we're waiting for our dinner to be delivered, I believe the Wine has breathed enough, so let's take it out to the Gazebo and relax a little before it arrives."

"Rachael, will we be able to hear the Doorbell out there?"

"Not to worry James, my Cell-phone is synced-up, and will sound off when the Doorbell rings, I can even talk to and see anyone at the door through the intercom using my phone."

"Nice! Isn't technology awesome, sometimes?"

"Yeah, sometimes!"

As they make their way down the rear stairs that takes them into the Backyard with James in the lead, with the Wine bottle in tow. With Rachael following not to close behind him, she experiences a quick dizzy spell and almost falls, but catches herself, before she goes down on her arse, proclaiming;

"Whoops! Almost fell on my arse, these damn new shoes, Love how they look. Hate how they feel."

"I've heard that from women before, will you ladies ever learn?"

They sit in the Gazebo, and James pours the Wine claiming;

"I've played in this Gazebo as a child, but this is the first time, I've ever drunk Wine in it with a Woman."

"I advise you to sip it, it packs a powerful punch!"

"Yeah, I know, when I was young, my Dad would always give Gabrielle, and me a small glass of it, at our family Holiday dinners, and even that small amount would make us a little loopy."

"By the way James, who knows that you stopped in Mystic on your way to Providence?"

"Not a soul, I do what I want, when I want! No one knows, that I'm even going to Providence. It's my business why and what for, no one else's."

As they sit, relaxed sipping their Wine, Rachael has to turn her face away from James, because her vision becomes faintly awash in a red mist, and then back to normal again, so she knows that her eye color is changing, and she doesn't want him to see it happening. As he tries to look her in the face, she keeps her face even more turned away from him.

James, finally asks of her,

"Rach, what are you, stretching your neck to look at?"

"Oh, nothing in particular. Do you see anything in your direction that seems out of place?"

As he turns to look in the opposite direction from her, she quickly turns toward him and sees that his neck is exposed to her, in the same moment she could hear and feel the rhythm of his Blood pumping slowly through his veins. In what seemed like minutes only took seconds, as her fangs extend, she lunges in at his neck, and at the same time, with the strength of many, she holds him fast, and proceeds, to partake of his life sustaining Blood as quickly as She possibly can, within seconds she sucks out two or three pints, and as he loses consciousness, goes limp, making his body lollop toward her, helplessly giving himself over, so now she can easily finish her first Human **Blood Passion** feasting. As she finishes the taking of his Blood from his body, and his heart stops beating, Rachael starts to feel a surge of exhilaration like never before, in any of her feedings on animal Blood. She throws her head back and relishes the new feeling of strength, and power. She then pauses in her revelation to remember what is written in her real Father's Memoirs about disposing of her victim's empty Carcass, and it quickly dawns on her about him pitching them off the Cliff and into the waters below, so that the undertow can take them away. She had always wondered how her real Father came to have the strength to accomplish this task, but as she easily lifts his lifeless body, she wonders no more, of how it was done, as She carries the lifeless body of James, she also gives thought to the fact that her Godmother Marlena, must have disposed of her victims bodies in the same fashion, after all, she surely read the Memoirs, and must have used them as a guide. Rachael stops short of the fence, puts the body down to remove any identification from it, unlatches the gate so as to get easy access, to the Cliff's Edge, then lifts up the body of the last, of the Varlino family, and raises it over her head, with an act of strength unimagined, only moments ago. She than hurls the body out far enough to clear the rocks. As it plunges into the water, in a cynical manner she requests;

"Say hello, to your Mother, for **me**!"

Chapter Six

RACHAEL TURNS ROUND, walks away from the Cliff's Edge without an ounce of remorse in her heart or mind, for what she has just done.

As she makes her way to the Gazebo she hears her Cell-phone signaling her from the Gazebo table where she had left it, that someone is at the front door. She surmises that it must be the food delivery from the Ebb Tide Restaurant, picks up her Cell-phone off the table, puts it on vibrate, then places it into her jeans back pocket, she continues to walk toward the back door to enter the house and make her way to the front, but stops short of the Kitchen door, takes in a deep breath, and concentrates just slightly harder than it takes to suppress her Blood feasting attributes, so that her eyes return to their normal color, and her fangs, and finger nails retract back to their Human state.

To have this much control, over this unique transition of her Vampiric **Blood Passion** of the ingesting of Human Blood, from just Blood feasting on animals brings a wry smile to her face.

In the first floor Bathroom just outside and to the right of the Kitchen archway, she tidies herself, clears any Blood from around her mouth, also makes sure that there isn't any Blood on her blouse, and continues to the front door, as she draws closer to it she sees through the cut glass oval on the door, two people standing in the foyer holding silver covered serving trays.

Rachael opens the door to greet the delivery people saying,

"Hello, thank you, you people are here right on time as usual please come in," She exclaims and continues motioning to the Sideboard, directing them, "You can put the trays down on the Sideboard, right there."

Rachael requests, as she quickly makes her way up the Grand Staircase to fetch some money for a healthy tip for them,

"Please give me a moment, I'll be right down!"

She returns momentarily, and hands each of them a twenty dollar bill, and also the tray and cover from the last delivery saying, "You can take back these from the last time." And notifies them, "Please be sure that they put this on my tab, and send be the bill for this month's deliveries as usual."

The delivery people agree, give her their thanks for the tips and leave the house. Not feeling hungry for food at the moment she leaves the trays where they are, enters the Library to possibly do some more writing of her Manuscript, she's unpleasantly surprised to find all the pages of her Father's Memoirs scattered all round the floor, with a puzzled demeanor she proclaims out loud,

"**What the…!**"

Rachael dumfounded by this, checks all the windows, but they are all closed and secure, so no wind could have done this and no one could have entered the room. She then stands in the middle of the room with her hands on her hips, and announces adamantly,

"Okay, who's screwing around with me?"

She waits a moment or so, but gets no reply, so she reiterates,

"Okay, so no one's going to fez up to doing this, fine, I can wait until you have the nerve to come forward."

With that said, she goes around, and picks up the pages, as she places them in order she says softly,

"It's a good thing my Father numbered the pages, or this would be a daunting task."

Just as she finishes the task, her Cell-phone vibrates in her pocket; she pulls it out to see that its Lucy calling. She rolls her eyes and answers it with,

"Hey Lucy, What up?"

"One more week!"

Lucy announces excitedly.

"Yeah, for what?"

Rachael replies agitatedly.

"Why the, house warming party, Rach!"

"Lucy I know, really I don't need a countdown!"

"Yeah, well, Bobby, tells me about two dozen plus, people from his school, have already told him they'd be coming."

"That's ta-riff'."

"Yeah, I think so!"

"And what about our friends, Lucy?"

"I've spread the word all over, and I've had several calls telling me that they'd be coming."

"Lucy, has Bobby secured the D.J. for the party, he hasn't told me yet, that his friend, Shane of 'MusicSmith' has been hired?"

"Bobby hasn't' told you? Yeah, that's all set, I don't know why he hasn't told you yet, oh wait, he told me to tell you, and I guess I just did!"

"Oh, Lucy, you're such a,… a,…"

"Rachael, I'm such a… a… what?"

"Lucy the Mailman's here I have to go, talk later, bye."

As she hastily hangs up, unheard by her Lucy says,

"Okay, Rach catch you later."

Rachael collects her mail, and she sees an official letter in the bunch, with excitement she opens it to see that it's the document, granting her the change of name from DeClerico to Valli.

She holds the letter up, raises her head and announces proudly, and loudly so that anyone within earshot can hear,

"I am now officially, my real Father's progeny, Michael Valli's spawn. His Daughter Rachael Valli!"

She lowers the letter down, along with her head, saying softly,

"In more ways than one, I'd have ta' say."

As she looks up and to her left, she spots the serving trays on the Sideboard, and realizes that she's still isn't hungry for food, so what to do with the dinners? She gives this some thought and comes up with;

I'll take the food out back, and leave it for the animals, after all many of them have died to supply me with a Blood feasting over the years of me growing up, so why not give something back.

She picks up the trays and makes her way out to the Backyard; she empties them on the ground far enough away from the Cliff fence, where the trees begin to get thick. Then goes to sit in the Gazebo to wait for the animals to come for it, while waiting she pours herself a glass of Wine from the bottle that is on the table, from before, her very first **Blood Passion** feeding took place.

She didn't have to wait long before two Raccoons show themselves; a rather large one, and a smaller one, but not small enough to be a baby, they both approached the dish with the beef in it, but the larger one hisses at the smaller, to bade it away, then turns its face to Rachael, she was a little taken aback by this because it had glowing red eyes, and unusually long fangs, it hisses at her. And then begins to consume the beef, the smaller one seems to be contended with the chicken meal. A rather large Seagull comes flying up, and over the fence, landing close to the large Raccoon to try to get some of the food for itself, this large, strange looking Raccoon quickly lunges at it, locks on to its neck; the gull immediately goes limp and seems to be dead. It appears to Rachael that it sucked out its Blood, like a Vampire of sorts.

She gives this some questioning thoughts;

Could there possibly be a Vampiric Raccoon roaming round Mystic?

That's rather strange, but look at me, thinking that something is strange, when I'm a Human Vampire in Mystic myself; the real question is how the heck did something like that come to be? Well, Rach, you just saw it so it must be true, seeing is believing, right? I just hope it won't be a problem for my guests at the party, but the noise and the number of people should keep it away, only if someone wanders off alone could there be a chance of a tragedy happening, I would have to guess.

When the Raccoons cease their eating, they carry off their left over portions into the woods, Rachael filled with curiosity, steps out of the Gazebo to where the Gull's body lays, examining it to find two small puncture wounds on its neck, and it does seem to her, that there is little to no Blood left in it's body. She carries it to the Cliff's Edge and pitches it into the water below. For the second time today, she closes the gate. Takes the unfinished bottle of Wine and the glasses from the Gazebo, with the sun just starting to set, she decides to call it a day and go in the Cliff House, thinking maybe she can figure out what happened in the Library, and why. If not, she could do some more writing on her Manuscript.

Chapter Seven

RACHAEL RETURNS TO the Library to happily find all is in order. She sits at the Desk, opens her Laptop and then her Manuscript and begins to write;

After a lovely dinner in a small, quaint, restaurant, downtown Mia and Marcus walk through the park, back to her apartment, where his Car is parked. As they walk slowly, hand and hand, she has thoughts of; I really don't know much about this new Man in my life, I do need to inquire about his past. As they continue to stroll along, with her in these heavy thoughts, suddenly, like out of no where, a cloaked figure is seen walking toward them.

This mysterious cloaked individual stops about ten feet in front of them, and proclaims in a deep guttural voice;

"Well Well, Marcus, look what you find here, in the big city!"

"Lucas this can't be a coincidence, surely you, are following me."

This cloaked Lucas pushes back his hood to reveal his face; Mia is totally shocked by what she sees.

Just at this moment Rachael is distracted by the Doorbell ringing, she saves her writing and goes to answer the door.

As she approaches the front door, she notices a small red Federal Parcel Delivery Vehicle parked out front, she buzzes the outside door to let the delivery person into the foyer, then opens the inside door, to be handed a parcel, as the delivery person says;

"A special delivery for you."

"Thank you so much!"

She answers with gratitude.

The driver proclaims as he leaves;

"Have a good night!"

And Rachael replies.

"And you also!"

She goes back to the Desk and sits to open the envelope with growing curiosity; she then pulls out the contents and is greatly excited to find a bill of sale, and title for the late Marlena's MG Automobile; and declares excitedly,

"All right! I now own a Car! Awesome! I will contact Bobby later to take me to the D.M.V. to get it registered for the road, and call the Insurance Company to open a Policy."

She then makes the attempt to get back to her writing saying aloud,

"Okay now, where was I, oh yeah."

And with that said, she returns to the writing of her Manuscript.

She sees something she has a hard time believing, this Man or whatever it is, has eyes that glow red, and very long eye teeth, that shine in the moon light! She asks,

"Marcus, who or what is this thing?"

"Mia, run, run home as fast as you can, I'll handle this!"

"But Marcus, I just can't run out on you, you may need….!"

Mia is cut off by Lucas saying,

"That's right honey, you stay, you just may be the leverage I could use."

"Mia, I said RUN, ***RUN NOW****!*

Marcus adamantly repeats.

She quickly steps in front of Marcus facing this intruder, putting herself between them.

"Mia, are you out of your mind! Get out of here, like I told you to!"

"Ah, Marcus, you've picked a rather perky one this time, doesn't matter, you're coming back to the Cabal with me."

Mia turns round to Marcus and inquires of him,

"Marcus, what is this Cabal, he wants to take you back to?"

Before Marcus can answer her, Lucas quickly closes the space between them, and now within reach of her, where he easily pushes her aside like a rag doll, she is slammed up against a large tree, and falls to the ground unconscious.

Marcus gestures to go to her, just as his own eyes turn red, and his fangs extend, putting him in his defensive mode. He turns to his antagonist and says,

"Lucas, I'm not going back with you, to become the leader of the Cabal, so you can go back, and tell Quintus he'll have to find someone else."

"Marcus, you know I can't return without you, so you either come back of your own accord or draped over my shoulders."

"So, it's another battle you want, because you finally beating me is the only way that you could accomplish, getting me to go back!"

"Marcus, please, do not be foolish, how many times do we have to do this?"

"Well, I'd have to say, as many times as it takes to convince, the old bastard that I want OUT!"

Once again her writing is interrupted by her Cell-phone ringing. She sees that it's her Me-Ma calling, with a silent huff answers it saying,

"Hello, Me-Ma how are you, and Granddad?"

"We are well my Dear, I'm calling to tell you that we received your telephone invitation to the house warming party, and that we will be attending but we can't stay long."

"That's fine, I'm kind of glad you called, I need to change the name on the house deed title."

"Whatever for, my Dear?"

"I've had my Surname, legally changed to Valli, so I believe it should reflect that on the title. Right?"

"Yes, I suppose you're right, I'll talk to my boss, he's a lawyer, remember? So he'll know what and how to go about it."

"Thank you Me-Ma, I'll see you and Granddad at the party."

"Yes, you will, see you then, all my Love, bye.

And with that they both hang up. Just as she places her Cell-phone down it rings, and she sees that this time, its Bobby calling.

She answers inquisitively,

"Hey, Bobby, what up?"

"Rach, did Lucy remind you to call a Party Service Company to supply the tables, chairs and a portable dance floor that you're going to need?"

"No. Was she supposed ta?"

"Yes, I told her to!"

"Well, she's such a scatter brain sometimes!"

"Okay, Rach, you need to call Party Time, got a pencil? I'll give you their number."

Rachael writes down the number and says,

"Okay, Bobby, I'll call them right away, thanks! We don't need to scold Lucy for not telling me. Okay? And bobby, by the way, I will need you, to take me to the D.M.V. tomorrow afternoon."

"Yeah, you got the stuff for the Car, cool, no problem, see you tomorrow afternoon, bye."

Rachael reciprocates, and slowly places her Cell-phone down as if it might just ring again at any second.

And thinks,

Maybe I should turn it off, so I won't be disturbed anymore today, or I'll never get this chapter finished.

"Okay right after I call this party stuff supplier, that's just what I, will have'ta do.

She then, places the call just in time before they close for the day, and makes the arrangements for the party stuff to be delivered and setup for the day of the party. Shuts her Cell-phone off and goes back to her writing.

Chapter Eight

STRETCHING HER ARMS over her head, she lets out a deep yawn, saying,

"It's early, but I'm feeling rather fatigued."

So Rachael decides that she should get some sleep, and get a fresh start in the morning, so she shuts down her Laptop and makes her way to the upstairs Bathroom before heading off to bed for the night.

Not very long after she falls off to sleep, she is suddenly awakened by a rather disturbing dream that seems more like a nightmare. She bolts straight up in her bed, breathing uneasy, sodden with sweat, and apprehensively proclaims,

"**MARCAS**!"

She reaches over to her right and turns on the lamp on her night table, and looks around her room and realizes it was a dream about the story in her Manuscript, grabs the notepad and pen on her bedside table, and begins to write down of what she can recall that was in her dream.

She swings her legs out from the covers and sits on the edge of her bed noticing that her room is illuminated by the moonlight coming through her windows, so she turns off the lamp, gets out of bed to change into some dry sleep wear.

Now sitting on the vanity chair she looks into the mirror and catches a glimpse of something moving quickly across the room behind her, but when she swiftly turns round to see what it is, she sees nothing. Sitting for a moment she softly calls out,

"Dad, is that you? Are you there?"

No sound comes out of the darkness.

Silently, she patiently sits in her moonlit Bedroom and waits hopefully, for a response to her query. But all she hears is a faint laughter that sounds Female in nature. Her initial thoughts are that if what she is hearing is for real, like her Father did, maybe Marlena is now haunting the Cliff house, if so then; this probably would solve the mystery of her Father's Memoir pages being disturbed in the Library. Rachael is not at all afraid that it may be Marlena's Ghost, for she feels, what possible harm can come to her from a Ghost, so she will ignore it, like when her little Brother Mathew, would bother her to get her attention, ignoring him he would eventually stop and go away.

She lets out a sigh, and makes her way back to her bed. Lays her head down on her pillow and softly lets out a breath saying,

"Goodnight, Godmother."

Morning comes to Rachael at about eight. She rises from her bed, puts on a T-shirt and jeans, stuffs the note from her dream in her pocket, takes her Cell-phone from its charging pad, placing it in her back pocket and goes to the Bathroom, and then down to the Kitchen for her Breakfast, on her way to the Kitchen as she passes the Library, she takes a quick look into it to see that all is well. At the table while eating her yogurt with fruit in it, she turns on the radio to get the latest weather report for the next few days, to see if it will cooperate for the party to be out in the Backyard. Sounds like it will, so she finishes her Breakfast, and goes to the Library to do some more writing.

Before sitting at the Desk to begin, she takes out her Cell-phone from her back pocket, and lays it on the Desk, then removes the note from her front pocket, looking at it, she is slightly puzzled at what she has written on it, and stops to try to remember what took place in her dream, as she slowly sits her memory kicks in, remembering what she saw in the dream, and begins to write;

Marcus now in his Vampyre Veneer, looks over to where Mia is lying motionless to see that Mia has been knocked unconscious, makes a start to go to her aid, when Lucas quickly moves on him with a left cross to the side of Marcus's head. Marcus goes down to one knee and looks up at Lucas and says,

"So, that's how it's going to be this time!"

"Well, I do believe that this Girl could play to my advantage. Wouldn't you say?"

"Yeah, maybe, because that's what you would need to best me." Marcus replies, as he stands to make a move away from where Mia is, putting some distance between them and her. As Lucas shadows Marcus, he says,

"You're not thinking of getting away from me, are you? Because that's not at all like you, to make a run for it."

"No, just can use a little more room, to take you down, is all."

In a defensive stance, Marcus takes a quick look around and motions to Lucas to make his move.

"Take me down?"

"Yes, take you down, like all the times before this. Don't you remember? Getting old, Lucas?"

"Not so old to deal with the likes of a pup, like you."

"Well, you're wasting time talking, come on make your move, or can you only give sucker punches these days?"

"I'll show **you***, who the sucker is!" He replies, as he throws a roundhouse punch, which Marcus avoids by ducking, then counters by rising straight up with the full force of his whole body, where his fist makes contact with a forcefully delivered uppercut to Lucas's jaw, sending him up off his feet and flat on his back, where he passes out.*

As he looks down at his fallen adversary and says,

"That was for Mia!"

Marcus now takes advantage of this lull in the action to quickly go over to Mia, scoops her up in his arms to make a beeline to her apartment to get her out of harms way. He'll make his way back to Lucas, when he accomplishes getting Mia to safety. He lays her down on the two step stoop at her apartment building front door, and as he turns away to get back to Lucas in the park.

Mia awakens, opening her eyes to catch him briskly walking away from her, she calls out to him in a shaky but loud tone,

*"Marcus? **MARCUS**... answer me!"*

As he's walking away from her, in the direction of the park, he hears her call out; and without turning round, he answers her adamantly with,

*"Mia please, stay put, I'll be **back**!"*

And with that being said he begins to run.

She sits herself up on the stoop; bends her head down, puts one hand on her head injury, and the other covering her face, she softly states and asks,

"What on earth, have I got myself involved in, this time?"

Rachael decides to take a break from her writing, looks at her Cell-phone on the Desk, and realizes that she's not turned it on yet, so she picks it up and reluctantly turns it on, while going to the Kitchen to get something to drink.

As her luck would have it, as she sips her soda, her Cell-phone rings, the caller I.D. showing her that it's Bobby.

She swallows, puts her drink down and then leisurely answers it saying,

"Hey, Bobby, what up?"

"Rach, I've someone with me I'd really like you, to meet today!"

"Oh, and who might that be?"

"My good friend, and your party D.J. Shane Smith of 'MusicSmith', he's in from New York City, may I bring him over this afternoon?"

"Sure, how about around two."

"Sounds boss, we'll see you then."

Rachael hangs up, and takes a large gulp of her soda and states;

"At this rate, I'll never get my novel finished."

CHAPTER NINE

RACHAEL OPENS THE Kitchen door, steps out onto the back porch, walks down the cement stairs into the yard. Walks over to and enters the Gazebo to sit, lets out a deep sigh, as she looks around the yard thinking,

I'm the mistress of all I survey, and the master of nothing, not even my own life. When I was younger, and even through my teen years, I'd never given much thought to my being a real living Vampire before, I just accepted it as my extraordinary way of living, not even confronted my Mother about it.

But, now that I've taken my first Human life, to fulfill, and give birth to my now acquired ***Blood Passion,*** *in which I've inherited from my Dear late Father, I've some mixed feelings about how to deal with this way of life now, and for the first time that I ever can remember, thinking about it this way. My life is changing, what other changes, can be in store for me?*

She rises from the chair to exit the Gazebo, walks over to the tree with the strange name 'Nightwing' carved in it, the one and only Memorial to her beloved late true Father, Michael Valli, she reaches up and places her hand on it, saying,

"Father, I do not blame you for this implausible way I must now continue my life, I Love you. It is my fate, and I must deal with it, just as you had too, and I **will** live it, to the best of my capabilities, dutifully reading and studying your Memoirs, it can be my, 'Vampires for Dummies' Manual. I Love ya Dad, and will forever."

As she takes her hand away from the tree, a tear drop rolls down her cheek. She wipes it away, straightens herself up, takes in a deep breath, and returns into the house, to freshen up, change her clothes, and gather the paper work and the money needed to get her newly appropriated Car registered.

When Bobby comes by with this Shane D.J. guy, at about two, she'll have them take her to the registry, and then treat them, to a late lunch at the Mystic Pizza Restaurant, as a thank you, for doing this for her.

She sits at the Library Desk and looks around the room thinking,

There isn't a thing in my life, or in this house that belonged, or reminds me of my late Dad. I'll call Me-Ma right now, and see if she can remedy this unattached feeling I have.

Picks up her Cell-phone she speed dials her Grandmother. Carmella answers on the second ring,

"Hello, sweetheart, nice of you to call."

"Yes, are you busy, Me-Ma?"

"No, Dear, you sound a bit troubled. Is there something wrong, sweetie?"

"Well, kind of."

"Whatever could be distressing you, my child?"

"Well… Me-Ma, I do know that my Dad spent a lot of his Boyhood here in the Cliff house, with your Mom and Dad, and then lived here himself for a spell, and with all that, I still don't have anything that belonged to him. I hope this doesn't sound dumb, but I really would like to have something of his, from when he was alive. You wouldn't happen to have something of his that I could have, do you?"

"My Dear sweet child, I understand how you feel, ah, let me think, oh, just a minute; I do have his Laptop Computer. Would that do, my darling?" I've never even opened it, or turned it on, as a matter of fact, it's still in its carrying case in the front hall closet."

"That would be totally, awesome! Would you bring it to me when you come down here for the party?"

"Of course, we'd be happy to, your Grandfather and I will definitely bring it to you and the paperwork for you to sign for the change of name on the Cliff house title. We'll see you then, we Love you, be well, bye."

"Love you guys tons, bye!"

Rachael hangs up, and joyfully reflects out loud,

"My real Dad's Laptop! It will be so fetch, to have the actual Computer that he wrote his Memoirs with, and if he's happened to have deleted it, I'm almost sure that Bobby will know someone that could recover deleted files for me. Yeah… so cool!"

Expectedly, the sound of Bobby's distinctive Car Horn sounds out front,

Rachael states sarcastically,

"Well, speak of the devil."

She proceeds to the front doors to open them; the inside door first, and then the foyer door, which will let them know that they are welcome to come in, she returns to the Library Desk chair to check what she has gathered of what is needed for the Registry of Motor Vehicles, and sits to await, their entrance.

Bobby enters the house first, stops just inside the inner door and calls out,

"Rach, Rachael where are you?"

"Bobby, I'm here in the Library, please come in, I'm just gathering what I'll need for the registry to put my Car on the road, won't take a second."

"Rach, I've got Shane… Shane Smith the D.J. with me, he's standing in the foyer waiting to come in."

Bobby turns right and enters the Library where Rachael is still seated at her Desk and inquires,

"What ya mean, what you'll need for the registry?"

"Don't you remember I told you yesterday about, you and Shane can take me there, and then I'd be more than happy to treat the two of you to a late lunch at the Mystic Pizza. That's okay, right?"

"Yeah, Rach sure I remember, totally that's doable!"

"Well, don't let him stay out there, tell him to come in!"

"Yeah, sure!" Bobby replies, and turns round to motion through the archway, to Shane to enter the house, as he crosses the threshold, Bobby puts up his hand to him as a sign for him to wait before entering the Library archway, turns back to Rachael at her Desk, and announces as he's still holding up his hand to Shane to wait, and proclaims,

"It gives me great pleasure to present to you, straight from the Big Apple, the number one D.J. in my world, Shane Smith of 'MusicSmith'!"

Bobby then waves him in.

Shane enters slowly saying to Bobby,

"Bobby, what's with the dramatic entrance?"

As Shane turns to look at Rachael, they lock eyes on each other; she is mesmerized, holding her breath and freezes at the first sight of this beautiful looking young Man standing in front of her. To her, he is the Man she has imagined somewhere in a dream as her first Lover.

Bobby looks at Shane, and then turns to his right to look at Rachael, then leans in to prop himself on the Desk looking at her, somewhat in a puzzled manner and says,

"Rach… Rachael… Rach… earth to Rachael! Come in?"

He gets very little response from her so he straightens himself up and turns to Shane and proclaims,

"I really hate to interrupt, what seems to be a magic moment here, but if we're going to the registry, we really need to make a move."

Rachael slowly lowers her head, shaking bringing her out of her mesmerized state, looks up and over at Bobby to answer him, as she rises from her chair with her paperwork in tow, and utters a bit bewildered,

"Oh… yeah… yes… Bobby, I'm sorry you're right, we'd best get going."

Chapter Ten

RACHAEL WITHOUT TAKING her eyes off Shane reaches to pick up a slice of Pizza from the serving tray in the middle of the round table, which the three of them are sitting at in the Mystic Pizza Restaurant. Bobby looks at Rachael and attempts to pose a question to her,

"Rachael!"

Once again, getting her attention away from Shane, is a little difficult, so he tries again a bit louder,

"**Rachael**?"

And it seems to work, she reluctantly breaks off her gazing at Shane and looks at him, and agitatedly replies,

"**Yes**, Bobby, what is it, **now**?"

"Rach, I would surmise you do have all the arrangements for the party made? I mean you do have the catering, and party stuff supplier, scheduled I trust."

Turning her head back to Shane seated on her right, she answers Bobby,

"Yeah yeah, that's all fixed for this Saturday night, I'm not our beloved ditsy friend Lucy!"

Rachael slowly puts down her slice onto her plate; continuing to look at Shane, she can't seem to stop herself from staring at this beautiful looking Man; she is totally taken with him, but at last finds the ability to ask him,

"Shane, tell me, where are you staying for the time you will be here in Mystic with us?"

"I have a room reservation waiting for me at the Ebb Tide Motel, they are expecting me to check in soon, and that's where one of the company vans is parked, with all the D.J. equipment with my rucksack for my clothing and personal stuff. Bobby came by the Motel to get me just before I went to check in, for our prearranged meeting to come to your place to meet you."

"Well now, that just won't do, we can't allow you to stay there, when I have more than enough room to accommodate you at the Cliff House,"

She looks over at Bobby at her left, to support her and continues adamantly,

"**Right**, Bobby, tell him he should stay at with m… I mean the Cliff House; after all, that's where he'll be working the party! It will be so much easier. Tell him Bobby, **tell him**!"

Bobby replies, supportably,

"Shane, I believe she has a point."

Answering them, he politely gives in,

"Well, okay, if I won't be too much trouble, I suppose that I could do that."

"So you'll stay with m… I mean at the Cliff House then?"

"Yeah, sure, why not, if you two insist, I feel that I can't or mustn't refuse your gracious Hospitality, but right now, I need to use the Men's Room, please excuse me for a moment."

With Shane away from the table now, Bobby reaches over to Rachael and gently takes her hand saying,

"Rachael what on earth is with you, ever since you laid eyes on him, you've been acting like a pathetic Love sick teenager?"

"Bobby, what are you talking about, I just think he's really nice, and rather gorgeous too! You sound like you're a bit jealous of him."

As he lets go of her hand, and sits back in his chair, Bobby irritatedly replies to her statement,

"**What! Me! Jealous!** Jealous of Shane! Yeah, all right, so he's a great D.J., number one in my world, and somewhat handsome, but I don't see anything else about him that's awfully outstanding."

"Yeah, but you are not looking at him through **my** eyes!"

Their conversation goes cold, as Shane reappears at the table where they finish their late lunch, or actually more like an early dinner, Rachael pays the bill and they head out to Bobby's Car, to go to the motel to cancel Shane's room reservation. After that is accomplished, Rachael and Shane, in his van, head off to the Cliff House to get him settled in.

Shane with his rucksack in tow over his shoulder follows Rachael up the Grand Staircase to the second floor hallway. Reaching the second floor landing, Rachael directs him down the hall to the Bedroom just passed hers', opens the door and says,

"Okay, here you go, I feel you'll be rather comfy in here, I hope you don't mind, but there are no locks on the Bedroom doors, only the Bathroom doors have locks on them, I hope that's okay with you."

"Yeah, that's fine; I really don't think that anything is looking to do me any harm here."

"Of course not, you'll be quite safe,"

She points back down the way they came and continues, "And speaking of the Bathrooms, the second floor one, is just down there, it is the first door on the right just after the stairs. So you get yourself settled in, I'm going down, to the Kitchen to make us some fresh Coffee; you are certainly welcome to join me when you are done here."

"That sounds terrific, I could use a cup of fresh Coffee, and we can talk about the setup for the party for Saturday night."

"Yeah, that will be fab!"

"Okay then, I'll see you down there, don't be long."

Rachael makes her way to the Kitchen, puts the Coffee on; while she waits for it to brew, she gets out two mugs and spoons, cream, and sugar, having the thought of,

Okay now, I have'ta get my emotional desires under control, before I make a fool of myself, any more than I already have today, but, oh my god, he's' just, so ***hot****!"*

Her thoughts are interrupted by Shane calling out to her, from the bottom of the Grand Staircase, as he looks round.

"Rachael, hello, where are you?"

She leans out from the Kitchen archway, to answer him and to show him where she is,

"Shane! I'm over here in the Kitchen, come on in and sit, Coffees' almost ready."

Before he enters the Kitchen he stops just outside at the archway, and notices a small door to his left, turns his head and points at it then turns back to Rachael with an inquiring look on his face. Rachael notices this and informally states,

"That's a water closet; it's the first floor Bathroom with only a sink and toilet, no tub or shower like upstairs."

"Good to know."

He thankfully states as he enters the Kitchen and takes a seat at the table and proclaims,

"Rachael, this house is quite large, and truly beautiful! You live here all by yourself? Please don't get me wrong, it really is a handsome place and quite majestic, like some of the old Mansions down where I grew up, I'm sure it must have a history all its own."

"Well, let me see, yes, it is quite big, and yes, I do live here alone. The history of this house, the Cliff House as it is known as, here in Mystic, is a rather long and sorted tale."

"Well, you'll have'ta tell me all about it, sometime."

Rachael notices that the Coffee is ready to be served, so she pours them both some, then replaces the Carafe to its station, sits back down at the table, slides the cream and sugar over to him and says,

"I'd Love to tell you the whole sorted story, sometime! Do you plan on spending more of your time with m… I mean us, here in Mystic?"

"I believe I'll really like to, if you wouldn't mind, that is."

"Oh no, I wouldn't mind at all!"

"In the morning light, I'd like to get a good look at the Backyard, so as to know, where I can set up, and get power for my equipment and also help to get your new license plates put on your Car."

"That will be great; I need to take it to the body shop to get it a new black paint job, because I really feel it will look so fetch in black with its' red interior than being totally red! Don't you think?"

"Yeah, that sounds really cool! I can follow you there, and be your ride back here."

"That will be perfect! You're so thoughtful."

And she adds in her mind,

And totally gorgeous, also.

"Well, it's the result of my Southern upbringing."

"Southern upbringing? Where are you, originally from?"

"Georgia, born and raised!"

"I'm not really that surprised, you surely don't sound or act like you're a person, from New York City; you will have to tell me, your story, sometime."

Shane mischievously replies,

"I do reckon, I could do that, Miss."

Rachael lets out a soft sexy giggle and says,

"I think we awe to get some sleep."

She rises to put the mugs and spoons in the sink, and the cream and sugar away, as Shane stands and agrees saying,

"Good night Rachael, see you in the morning, and thanks again for letting me stay here at the Cliff House. Sweet dreams!"

With that Rachael utters,

"Yeah, and you as well, really no need to thank m… I mean us, we're totally thrilled to have you here!"

And as she watches him depart the Kitchen, she has a pleasant erotic thought,

I'm quite sure, my dreams will be very sweet, if they are of you.

Chapter Eleven

RACHAEL IS HAVING a difficult time falling off to sleep, she keeps tossing and turning. Frustratedly gets out of bed, wearing her baby blue silk Croptop Camisole set; that her Mother gave her on her last Birthday; anxiously pacing back and forth at the foot of her bed, holding her arms across her chest. Finally, sitting at her vanity table, looking closely at herself in the mirror; letting out a deep sigh, and questions,

"What the heck is going on with me? I can't stop thinking of Shane, and what it might be like to make mad Love to him! It would be my first time; I can only hopefully imagine it would be incredible!"

Picking up her hair brush to fix her shoulder length light brown hair, suddenly from an undetermined place in the room hearing what sounds to her like a fairly familiar Woman's voice whispering softly,

"Go for it."

"Hello! What did you say?"

She leans even closer into the mirror, to look at the room behind her and sees nothing or no one.

The voice speaks again,

"You heard me. I know what you what to do. **Oh, just do it**!"

Rachael quickly spins round in her chair and firmly answers and asks,

"How do you know what I want to do? And who are you anyway?"

"Who, or what, I am doesn't matter, what matters is that you only go round once in life, so don't waste any opportunities, because they usually don't come round again."

"And you know all this because?"

"Because in **my** lifetime, I had too many missed opportunities! Missed opportunities turn into regrets! Enough talk, your wasting time Girl, go to him. **Now**!"

"Ah, wait... what if he rejects me?"

"With his gentlemanly demeanor, he may make an effort to at first, but when you bring on your feminine wiles coupled with your sexual desires, you will ultimately win him over, getting what you desire and most likely crave, from this Man you definitely have strong feelings for."

"Well, I'm not actually sure, that **I** will be able to accomplish it."

"My Dear, it's not **you** that will be making it happen, it's your pent up Human emotions, they will take you over, just open to them, let them escort you to a place inside you that you're never have been to before! Believe you me, it will be wonderful!"

"Will I feel any regrets, after this act?"

"No, not at all, if you are really feeling genuine Love for him."

"How will I know that?"

"Young lady, you are wasting time, like I said before, **just do it**!

"And just how would you surmise, that I go about it?"

"First, freshen your perfume, and go softly now to his bedside, slide in slowly and gently beside him, the sensation of your warm body against his will comfort him and he should open to you. As you feel him slowly awaken, and surrender to you, with a soft exhale in his ear, whisper his name."

"And that will work?"

"Yes, it has many times for me, now stop wasting time and **go**!"

"Okay okay, I'm going I'm going!"

She rises from the vanity chair and adorns herself with the short Robe at the foot of her bed that matches her Croptop Camisole, slides into her favorite Silk Slippers, and goes out into the hallway.

As Rachael slowly makes her way down the hall toward Shane's' Bedroom door, for some strange unknown reason, not at all troubled about, or frightened of, whom it was that she was being encouraged by in her Bedroom, she has a more pressing fixation inhabiting her thoughts, such as; gettin' with this Man that has highly stimulated her emotions and sexual desires.

Just short of reaching his door, sitting in one of the hallway chairs to consider her actions, one final time.

Am I going about this the right way, shouldn't I wait, maybe till after the party to attempt this?

The voice from her Bedroom enters her thoughts,

There's really no time like the present! Just do it, you're feeling it now so go with it! Trust me, it will be fine.

Rachael answers softly out loud,

"Trust you? I don't even know who you are!"

Back in her head she hears,

Okay, one more time, who I am doesn't matter, I know, and can feel what you what and need, this is the perfect time.

Rachael lightly slaps her thighs and softly says,

"Okay, I'll do this, or should I say we? Since when as logical thinking ever stoped me from getting what I want and it won't this time either."

We? This is where my interference ends; you will enter this endeavor without me.

"Thanks for the privacy."

Rachael softly proclaims, as she slowly opens Shane's door. The light of the full moon coming through the undraped windows illuminates the room, with the sheet only covering half his body as he lies on his side facing away from her, seeing that he sleeps naked.

Rachael moves catlike to the side of the bed close to her, and quietly removes her slippers, robe and panties. Then smoothly slides in to spoon with him, as she does this, he instinctively detects the heat of her body against his, which makes him stir a little, without moving he lets out a soft incoherent murmur,

"Oh, Cher... !"

Rachael is really too involved in her seduction of him to take notice of what he uttered, she then lifts up to be at his ear, tenderly lets out a long exhale, softly and seductively, declares,

"Shane, take me."

He responds to this, by awakening without opening his eyes, he slowly turns in her direction, she gently takes hold of his cock, and begins to softly fondle and stroke it, making it enlarge and get hard in her hand. He reacts to this stimulation by gently caressing her breast. They mutually engage in an intensely deep kiss.

As their long passionate first kiss comes to an end, they slightly part, only then does he open his eyes, to see her lovely face illuminated by the moonlight, slightly surprised, but happily sees that it's Rachael, that he's about to make Love with, he softly says her name,

"Ah, Rachael."

He crushes her against him with another intense kiss; his right hand makes contact with her now wet pulsating sweet pussy, telling him that, she's ready to receive him. At first he finds it a bit difficult to enter her, revealing to him that this will be her first time, enlightening him that she's a virgin, even so, he's now utterly flooded with sexually stimulated desire. He ultimately makes penetration, Rachael moans in slight discomfort, and then lets out a sound of total delight, hearing this he kisses her again, but gently this time, to induce comfort to her.

After an uncountable amount of time, for they are totally consumed with one another, when mutual bliss has been attained, they lie on their backs side by side, hand and hand, both of them breathing a bit uneasy, and sodden with sweat.

They turn to each other, kiss, embrace, and no sooner fall into deep restful sleep.

Chapter Twelve

SHANE AWAKENS TO find Rachael is not in bed with him, he gets out of bed, puts on his briefs, T-shirt, jeans and socks, to quit the Bedroom in search of her. Peering out the Bedroom door into the hallway, he calls out,

"Rachael?

He waits a moment for an answer, but none comes. Figuring that she might be in the Bathroom just down the hall, he softly knocks at the door asking,

"Rach, excuse me, are you in there?"

Once again he gets no reply, and then realizes that if she was in there, she probably would have heard him the first time when he called to her from his Bedroom door.

He resigns himself from searching every room on the second floor, and a set of stairs leading up to what might be a third floor, so he decides to go downstairs. Once at the bottom of the Grand Staircase, he looks to his left, into the archway entry into the Library, and still no Rachael. He looks round puzzled, then hears noises coming from the direction of the Kitchen. He calls out one more time,

"Rachael?"

She pops her head out from the Kitchen, entry archway, and declares, smiling with delight,

"Shane, my Love, you're up! Good, come, sit, have some Breakfast with me! Coffee has just finished brewing and is ready to be served. Hope you like bacon with your eggs?"

Shane enters the Kitchen; while Rachael's filling two mugs of Coffee on the counter she finishes her query.

"If not, I could cook up some sausages if you'd rather!"

"No no, bacon will be great on the crispy side, like my eggs over easy, please. I truly do appreciate all you're doing for me."

"And I... **really** appreciate what you did for me last night!"

She states mischievously.

As he takes a seat at the table, he looks out at the Backyard through the back windows and notes,

"Rachael, it looks like a nice sunny day, after we eat I'd like to go out back and have a look round, to know where I'll be setting up for the party, and like I mentioned yesterday, I'll be needing power."

"Well, you can get all the power you'll need from the garage. Will that be okay?"

"I believe so; we always carry plenty of extension cords with our D.J. equipment, in the van. And after that's finished I'll put your new plates on your Car for you. Do you have any tools in the house?"

"Yeah, such as?"

"Well, probably a screwdriver of some kind."

"Okay, should be some in the tool drawer," She points over at the counter, "Right there."

"Great, sounds like a plan!"

The next few days before the party, goes by with them spending all their time in each others company. Shane follows her to the Mystic paint and body shop to leave her Car for the new paint job, then they go for a ride round Mystic in his company van, with Rachael as his personal tour guide, they eat at the Mystic Pizza Restaurant once again, and stroll down Main Street, just enjoying being together, where they run into a few people who are planning to attend the party, and also bump into Lucy and she is totally awed with Shane. And a day spend at the Mystic Aquarium. Their nights are spent in each others arms, making Love.

The morning of the day of the party, after Breakfast Rachael calls Lucy, before Lucy can call her. Lucy answers her call with;

"Hey hey, Rach, it's the **big** day! What color are you wearing I wouldn't want to clash with you!

"Lucy, don't be silly about what color I'm wearing, doesn't matter. Wear whatever color you want, just wanted to remind you that I'll need you, to come here a little early, you being my Co-hostess after all."

"And what time would that be?"

"About four, but no later, we'll need to talk."

"What! About your dreamy Shane?"

"No! Please, don't be silly. About the party rules."

"Rules! There'll be rules?"

"Of course, we need to be considerate of my neighbors!"

"Oh yes, you're right, the loud music you mean."

"That, yes, Lucy and checking that our guests don't get to rowdy and wander off my property."

"Maybe, Rachael, we should have a Police presents?"

"Could we do that? Or are you just being your usual silly self?"

"Just being silly! I'll have my Dad bring me over a little before four, bye, see you then!"

As Rachael hangs up, Shane stops taking inventory of his D.J. equipment in the garage, and inquires of her,

"Was that the Lucy, your silly Girlfriend that we ran into on Main Street the other day?"

"Yeah, she can be quite the ditz at times, but I do Love her, we've known each other since like forever. I was thinking of giving her my Scooter, over there, for her Birthday, now that I have my own Car, really don't need it anymore."

"Sounds like a real nice thing to do for her Birthday. When are you suppose ta' get your Car back?"

"Rob, the owner of the shop said, it should be ready, about the middle of next week, he'll call me, I'm sure."

"Sounds like good timing for me to take you there; I do need to get back to the Big Apple on Friday afternoon for a club job over the weekend, and then I'll rush right back here to you on Sunday afternoon."

"That sounds super; I'll be waiting here with baited breath, to be back in your arms once again!"

Just about three thirty, a large van pulls up at the front of the Cliff House, Rachael, and Shane walk down the driveway to see who it is, to find that it's the party supply company. A person that seems to be the leader exits the van, and greets them with a question,

"Good afternoon, are you Rachael Valli?"

"Yes, I am."

"We're here to set up for your party."

"Okay,"

She answers them, and turns to Shane, and states,

"You'll need to give them the driveway."

Shane responds,

"Of course, I'll move my van, straight away."

"Good, then we can get started; by the way, did my boss tell you about our new noise dampening equipment that you can rent, so as not to disturb your neighbors?"

"No, she didn't. What's that all about?"

"Well, for a small extra rental fee, we can set it up at the front yard of your house, and any and all noises coming from the party, whether inside the house or out, will not be heard by your neighbors."

Rachael inquires,

"Is it a large and cumbersome apparatus?"

"Oh, no, not at all, it's practically invisible!"

"Okay then set it up."

After the setup for the party is completed, Shane begins to set up and test his D.J. equipment, just as he finishes his testing of it, Rachael requests of him,

"Shane, since my Parents with my Brother, and my Grandparents should be arriving early, please play some soft music to start with. Okay?"

"Of course Rach, will do."

Lucy, arrives just as the party decorations are finished being installed, seeing them, proclaiming with total excitement,

"The party supply people did an awesome job, all the pretty lights and decorations they have strung will look so fetch, once it gets dark!"

"Yeah, Lucy and all the tables, and chairs close to the dance floor look, great!"

"So like you declared; 'this should be the party of the year!'

Lucy excitedly retorts,

"Should? It **most** definitely will be, Rachael!"

She then turns to Shane, asking him,

"What do you think?"

He replies,

"Oh yes, most definitely!

Michael Sr. and Carmella Valli, arrive at the Cliff House party slightly after four, as they said they might. Rachael greets them both with an embrace and a kiss, quickly introducing them to Shane, her party D.J. and new Beau. Carmella hands Rachael her real Father Michael Valli Jr.'s Laptop, thanks her and quickly takes it into the House putting it on the Desk in the Library.

Rachael swiftly returns to the Backyard and apologizes that the Mystic Pizza mobile catering truck, that has recently arrived, is not ready to serve any food yet, but she does offer them refreshment, they agree to a soda, and then announce they must be going. Kisses of goodbye are exchanged and they take their leave.

Now being a little after five o'clock Rachael's Mom; Mina, her half Brother, Mathew and her Stepfather, Joseph arrives, an introduction is made to Shane. And Lucy greets them respectively as usual.

Rachael is than told by the Pizza chef that the first Pizza is ready to be served; Matthew over hearing this, impatiently grabs a paper plate and a soda, but is warned by Mina about him burning his mouth, if he doesn't wait for the slice of Pizza to cool a bit. Shane plays some nice soft slow music, so Mina and Joseph can have the first dance of the party.

Chapter Thirteen

AFTER MINA, AND Joseph finished their dance, they advise Rachael's Brother Mathew, that they must leave now to be in time to get him to his Little League Baseball game. Not long after they go, the party guests begin to arrive, just a few at first, as the smell of freshly cooked Pizza went wafting out into the air of the Backyard, and into the neighborhood. Tantalizing some of the people nearby to exercise their invitations to come over for the party to wish Rachael a happy house warming and have some Pizza, and enjoy the music. One of them politely proclaims to Rachael,

"Rachael, if it wasn't for the superb smell of Mystic Pizza wafting through the neighborhood, we wouldn't have realized and remembered that you were having your house warming party this evening, we couldn't hear any noise at all coming from here!"

Rachael explains about the noise dampening devise temporarily installed, for the consideration of her neighbors.

She is sincerely thanked by them all for her thoughtfulness.

A little while after her neighbors take their leave many of the other friends of Rachael, Lucy and Bobby arrive, taking notice of the younger guest arriving, Shane cranks up the music for them to dance and enjoy.

The party went on for a while without incident or trouble,

Rachael contributed it to the fact that no alcoholic beverages were being served or aloud, but as the music volume lowered, suddenly a Blood curdling scream was heard coming from the thickly wooded area to the declining side of the property. Rachael made a quick scan of the party and did not see Lucy. Once again a scream rang out in the name of Rachael; Rachael immediately recognizes the voice of her best and long time friend, Lucy. She then makes a mad dash in the direction of it, she brings out her highly sensitive Vampire senses of hearing and smell, as she does this Lucy runs right into her, in a panic, breathing heavily and erratically. Rachael tries to calm her and inquires,

"Lucy, whatever is the matter?"

"Oh, Rach there's a Monster thingy out there!"

"A what? A Monster out where?"

Lucy points back in the direction she came and says,

"Out there, on your land!"

"Lucy get back to the party, and stay there, we'll talk about why you were out here, later!"

"What are you going to do?"

"I'm going to find your Monster thingy!"

"Well then, I'm going with!"

"Oh no you're not, get back to the party. Lucy that's not a request it's an order, now go!"

As Lucy turns round and heads back to the party, she grumbles under her breath,

"I never get to have any fun."

Rachael waits a moment, to be sure that Lucy is at a safe distance away from her and any danger, and cannot see her, brings out her full Vampire attributes, because she feels strongly that Lucy's Monster thingy is, her inhabitant Mutated Vampire Raccoon, her very own resident evil, in which she figured someday she'd have to deal with, so she reflects, as she carefully walks in the path that her heightened senses direct her to.

I guess, today's the day, or should I say the night.

Lucy gets back to the party, where she is greeted by Shane, and he frantically asks of her,

"Lucy, are you okay? Where's Rachael? Why is she not with you?"

"She went, to confront what just about scared the life out of me!"

Shane anxiously replies,

"She what? Oh my Lord, is she **crazy**?"

"That's just what I was thinking too when I tried to…!"

"I'll need a Flashlight," Shane interrupts, as he turns and quickly runs to the house to get one, and under his breath, he continues, "What a time, to not, have my Guns with me!"

As Shane comes back with a Flashlight to the place that he left Lucy, Rachael begins to appear from the woods holding her arm that is bleeding. Shane and Lucy both rush to her,

Shane proclaims,

"Rachael you're bleeding!"

Rachael replies snidely,

"Ya think?"

Shane turns to Lucy as he helps Rachael get to the house,

"Lucy, run to the house and fetch the first aid kit from the Kitchen, on top of the Fridge!"

"I know where it is!"

"Then go now, quickly and get it before Rachael bleeds to death!"

Once at the house, in the Kitchen, Shane bandages the wound to stop the bleeding. Rachael now seated at the Kitchen table, Shane turns to Lucy and tells her to go back to the party and tell all the guests that everything is okay. He then confronts Rachael about what happened to her out in the yard. She plays it coy, and just tells him that she tripped on something in the dark and cut her arm in the fall. He only half believes her, but considering her present state, he doesn't what to press the issue right now, maybe she'll tell him what exactly happened later or tomorrow.

"You can stop fussing over me now; I'll be fine, now please get back out there and get the music back on so my party can continue!"

"Okay, but I think you should go to the Hospital and get that looked at, you probably could use a stitch or two, or three, or…

"Shane, really my Dear, I Love your concern for me but it's already stopped hurting, now will you please, stop doting over me and get back to the party, I'll be just fine, and be out in a minute, there's something I want to look at in the Library!"

She enters the Library, sits at her Desk, clumsily opens her Father's Laptop and impatiently waits for it to come up.

Chapter Fourteen

RACHAEL ANXIOUSLY SEARCHES through her Father's Laptop hoping to find a folder with his Memoirs in it.

Just might be more in it than is printed out before he was gone. She happens upon a folder entitled my Memoirs and gets a feeling of exhilaration, double clicks it only to find that it's empty, with a sigh of disappointment she sits back in her chair. As the wound on her arm begins to pulsate in rhythm with her heart. Sadly, she takes in a deep breath and calms herself thinking as she exhales,

I guess I'll need Bobby's friend that can retrieve deleted files. I believe he said he'd be bringing him to the party.

Rachael slowly rises from her chair to avoid any possible dizziness that might come over her, after standing for a moment she closes the Laptop, and rejoins the party. All who approach her to see about her condition are consoled by her words that she's all right, with a thank you for their concern about her wellbeing. Bobby greets her with an introduction to his friend from college, Ryan, whom she remembers that, Bobby had told her about, as the person that should be able to retrieve deleted files from a Computer.

She gently shakes his hand, leans into his ear and softly declares,

"If what Bobby tells me about your Computer skills is true, I'll be in need of them, and will gladly pay you for your efforts in trying to accomplish what I want to do with his… I mean my Laptop

Computer, whether or not you succeed in what I require for you to do."

Ryan replies with,

"Well, sounds rather intriguing, I'll definitely be at your service as soon as possible, we'll need to schedule a meeting. I'll have Bobby give you my Cell-phone number before the night is over."

"That sounds fab! Now please have yourself some delicious Mystic Pizza and enjoy the party."

"Thanks, I will."

Bobby walks up to Rachael and caringly inquires,

"Rach, what happened to your arm?"

"Oh, you noticed the bandage!"

"How could I not? I saw it when you shook Ryan's hand."

"Well, yeah, I took a little fall, I'll be fine, and please you go have some Pizza and some fun, now. After all, part of all this was your idea."

"Yeah, it was, wasn't it? So it's Pizza and fun time! I'm gone!"

Rachael sits in one of the many chairs around the dance floor and watches Shane do his thing at his portable D.J. table, she has a concerning thought about having him in her life and keeping him safe from her **Blood Passion**.

The party continues on without any other incidents, at close to the time for the Mystic Pizza mobile truck to shut down, they request of Shane to make the announcement, that the last of the Pizzas are available for the night, almost like a last call at a bar. With that, some of the guests begin to leave, giving their thanks to Rachael for the Pizza and sodas, and Shane for the great music, he gives them his unique repose of,

"Thanks… Kool Beans!"

The rest of the remaining guests begin to leave as the Pizza truck packs up and leaves. After just about everyone are gone, including Lucy, Bobby, and his friend Ryan. As Shane packs up his gear, Rachael slowly walks to the back door, pauses to look out at the area of the Backyard where Lucy's Monster thingy was supposed to have been, noticing two small red points of light, out in the dark about five feet off the ground, determinedly reflecting,

Another time my resident evil fiend, another time!

The week that follows goes by without incident, mostly routine things like some light shopping, laundry, and house cleaning. Shane makes contact with the New York office, to confirm this upcoming weekend gig at the N.Y.C. Dance Club for the regular D.J. who's taking a vacation.

Thursday morning at Breakfast Shane explains to Rachael,

"Rach, honey, I will need to drive back to New York City tonight, for the club gig over the weekend, I can get back here on Sunday morning. Will that be okay with you?"

Rach takes a moment to think before replying,

That will work out good; I'll be needing a Blood feeding over the this coming weekend, so that put Shane out of harms way, for this one anyway.

Shane leans into her and says,

"Rachael are you there? Rach?"

She comes out from her thoughts and answers him,

"Oh, my yes, that will be fab!"

She then continues in her thoughts,

I'll call that friend of Bobby's, Ryan, and see if he can do the Computer thing for me on Friday, and if he can, after that is done, I'll then make a trip to Hartford, or Providence and find a victim like my Father wrote about doing in his Memoirs, I'll just follow exactly what he did, probably Friday or Saturday night.

As Shane stands to put his Breakfast things in the sink, he announces,

"Rach, I'm going out back and secure my mobile equipment, I won't need it in New York. Can I leave it here in the garage?"

Rachael once again is awoken from her thoughts and answers him vaguely, as he exits the Kitchen out to the Backyard.

"Yes of course you can.

After Shane quits the Kitchen and alone now she makes the call to Ryan. He answers his Cell-phone on the fourth ring, Rachael anxiously speaks first,

"Hello, Ryan? It's Rachael from the party last weekend."

"Yes, I remember!"

"Sorry for the short notice, but can you come and do the Computer thing for me tomorrow?"

"Well, what exactly is it that you want me to do?"

"I need you to retrieve some deleted files!"

"Yeah, I could probably do that for you, but I have no Car to get to your house in Mystic from mine here in New London."

"You can take public transportation to Main Street and I can come and get you, and bring you to my house."

"Where, on Main Street, should I meet you?"

"Out in front of, the Mystic Square Bookshop."

"Is that the one sort of across the Street from the Mystic Pizza Restaurant?"

"Yeah, that's the one, shall we say two o'clock?"

"Okay, two o'clock."

"Good, see you then."

And they both hang-up.

***

At their agreed upon time on Friday, Rachael arrives at their prearranged meeting place on Main Street, Ryan is sitting on the bench out front of the shop, she beeps her horn and waves him over to her Car. He gets in, and makes mention of what a cool Car she has, thanking him they speed off to the house. As they come over the low rise on Cedar Lane, he gets his first daylight look at the Cliff House, he is rather impressed with it and makes mention of it being a beautiful place.

Ryan if we get finished with the Computer stuff and you have no other plans, we can have some dinner together before you need to get back, I'll order us a meal delivered from the Ebb Tide Restaurant and we can eat out back in the Gazebo.

Ryan answers her agreeably,

"Yeah, that would be awesome; I've heard their food is the bomb, and I have no need to rush off back to New London, I've no plans with anyone, as a matter of fact, no one even knows I'm here."

Chapter Fifteen

RACHAEL AND RYAN exits the Car, and walk into the Backyard to the back door where they enter into the Kitchen. Ryan takes a seat at the table, as Rachael asks,

"Ryan, can I get you something to drink, a soda or maybe some juice?"

"Ya got a Cola?"

"I've Pepsi left over from the party. That okay?"

"Yeah, that'll be fresh!"

Rachael takes a seat at the table and slides him the can of soda, as she sips her grape juice.

Ryan enquires,

"So what exactly, is it you need my Computer skills for?"

"Ah, yes, I have a friends' Laptop, and would like you to recover some deleted files for them. You can do this for me?"

"I can certainly give it a try."

"Okay then I'll go get it."

Rachael enounces, as she stands up and leaves the room to go to the Library to get the Laptop.

She returns, in a moment, with it and puts it down in front of him asking,

"Will it take long?"

"All I can tell you right now is that it will take as long as it takes. Okay?"

"Yeah, whatever!"

Ryan works on the Laptop for a while, as Rachael is off doing laundry and some house cleaning. Just as she gives a thought to maybe get back to writing more on her novel, Ryan calls to her from the Kitchen.

"Rachael!"

"Be there in a mo!"

As she enters the room, asking,

"Making any progress?"

"Yeah, I think so. There's some files that were deleted some time ago, I do believe I can retrieve them for you."

"Sounds cool, go ahead."

Just as she finishes her response; the Clothes Dryer buzzes the signal that it's finished.

"Gotta get that, be right back."

As she gets the last load of clothing out of the dryer, and takes them to her room to be folded and put away.

Ryan opens the recovered files, and starts to read them, astonished at what he reads he sits back and thinks out loud,

"Wow, this is one amazing story, this Michael guy that used to live here some time ago turned into a Vampire and starts killing people. If it's true I should take this to the authorities or maybe make myself a copy with the Flash Drive I always carry with me. Might be able to sell the story, and make myself some bucks."

Unknown to him, Rachael over hears him, stopping short just outside the Kitchen archway, and thinks,

I can't let him do that with my Father's Memoirs, looks like I just found my next ***Blood Passion*** *feeding. Well, better him, than my Shane.*

She enters the Kitchen and naively poses the question,

"How's it going?"

"Good, I've got the files opened, and the subject matter is really some bizarre stuff and rather disturbing."

"Why, whatever do you mean?"

"They're about some guy that lived here a while ago; he became a Vampire in an incredibly extraordinary way. If this is a true account of an actual event, that really happened here than it should be taken to the Police or the FBI. What do you, think?"

"I think I'll need, to read what you found first, before I can make any decision about, what to do with it."

"Okay, go ahead I need to use the Bathroom."

"The small door to the right just outside the Kitchen archway is a water closet with a sink and a toilet."

Rachael directs him.

"Yeah, thanks."

As he rises from his chair she asks of him,

"Did you get **all,** of the deleted files?"

"Yes, I believe I did."

He answers her, as he's closing the door to the Bathroom.

Rachael thinks closing the Laptop,

Okay, so he's given me what I ***wanted*** *from my Dad's Laptop, now he can give me what I* ***need*** *from him.*

Rachael gets the Ebb Tide Restaurant menu out and sits herself on the couch in the Living Room. As Ryan quits the Bathroom and sees her sitting there, she inquires,

"I would think you're hungry by now, so come sit and pick out what you want to eat and I'll call for a delivery. It's the least I can do for your services."

As he sits down next to her, she hands him the menu, and he takes a look and decides at a glance that he'll have a Sirloin Steak.

"Good choice! Yeah, me too, with a baked potato, how do you want yours cooked? I like my steak rare."

"Medium rare for me, and I'll have a baked potato too."

Rachael takes out her Cell-phone and makes the call to place their order.

"It usually takes about an hour or so, for the food to arrive, would you care to go out back, and sit in the Gazebo with me and have some Wine? We can eat there and watch the sun go down together."

"That sounds totally fab!"

"Good, you go, and get yourself comfortable out there and I'll get us a nice bottle of Wine from my Wine cellar."

As Ryan makes his way out back, he sarcastically thinks,

A bottle of Wine from **my** *Wine cellar, and dinner while watching the sunset, boy, this chick is really asking for it.*

Rachael arrives with the Wine and two large glasses at the Gazebo, and hands the bottle and opener to him. He opens it and pours saying,

"This really is some place you've got for yourself here, great House, ocean view, your own Wine cellar. How do you do it?"

"I'll not bore you with my story, please have some Wine. Shall we toast your job well done?"

"I don't see why not."

They clink glasses, trying to make a showing of macho-ism, he takes a large swallow of Wine, unbeknown to him, that it's the Wine from Europe that's much more potent than any Wine that can be obtained here. He hastily sits back and proclaims,

"**Woo**! This Wine has some kick to it."

"Too strong for you?"

"No!"

He answers her, tips up his large glass to his mouth emptying it. He than swoons dropping his glass, and lollops back in his chair, just about passing out. As he's somewhat out of it, Rachael quickly brings out her Vampire attributes, turns his head toward her, and sinks her fangs into the right side of his neck, instantly sucking out about two pints of his Blood making him completely black out, now becoming her helpless victim of her **Blood Passion**.

Once again, she must now dispose of another lifeless body, so before her strength of many can leave her, she goes to the Cliff's fence gate opens it, and then back to the Gazebo to get the corpse, after emptying what's in his pockets onto the Gazebo table, carrying the body to the Cliff's Edge, lifts it up over her head, and declares sarcastically,

"Thank you, so much for your services, the one you knew about, and the one you didn't, and never will."

With that said, just as she's pitching this empty vessel out clearing the rocks, to let the ocean undertow do the rest.

Chapter Sixteen

RACHAEL RETURNS TO the Gazebo to find that her **Blood Passion** feeding was very efficient; there is no spilled Blood to clean up. So she sits for a moment to reflect on what just happened,

I now have two weeks until my next ***Blood Passion*** *feeding is needed, so my Love, Shane is safe for that long once again. How long can it go on this way? I do not think he will understand my curse, and be able to live with me having to kill to survive. Confronting him with it, will be out of the question, which means I will not be able to keep him in my life or tell him the real reason he will have to go. I'll have to come up with some silly Female reason for him to go, him not knowing the real reason will hurt him, but it will probably save his life. It will break my heart to lose my first and, presumably real Love of my life.*

Her thoughts are interrupted by the sound of her Cell-phone signaling that someone is at the front door. She leaves the Gazebo to enter the house to answer it, thinking,

Another meal for the wildlife.

At this time she stops, and has an idea about the Vampire Raccoon that she confronted the night of the party,

Maybe I can use the food as bait to draw it out, and destroy it, once and for all. After all, it did show itself before for food and if it does this time, I'll feed on it before it can, or could feed on me.

Rachael answers the door, and completes the food delivery transaction like so many times before. Out in the Backyard, she nonchalantly places the food where the trees begin to get denser, then stealthily backs off to hide herself behind the Gazebo, she now brings out her Vampire powers of heighten hearing, smell, speed and strength and waits to spring her trap. A few minutes go by, she begins to get anxious, so she springs up onto the Gazebo roof – where she lays as flat as possible so as not to be seen – acquiring a better view of the whole Backyard, plus to be able to launch herself on her adversary from above. After laying there for a few moments she realizes that the wind is blowing in the direction, so that the scent of the food she laid out, is coming at her, and not into the wooded area where the animals hide from view, at the same time her Cell-phone vibrates in her back pocket, signaling her that someone is at her front door, she will now have to get down from the roof to answer it, as beginning to do so, she hears Lucy call to her, from the foot of the back Staircase,

"Rachael, what the heck are you doing on the Gazebo roof?"

Rachael sadly realizes that her efforts to confront her rival are ruined for now; she'll have to find another way to confront this problem. She drops slowly from the roof just about floating to the ground; with a grunt she turns round walks over toward the back stairs to confront Lucy with,

"Lucy, you weren't suppose ta be here till five!"

"Yeah, I know, but, Jason and I finished up early at the Library, so I thought it would be okay to come here, right after we were done with our stuff. It is, isn't it?"

"Yeah yeah, I guess so. Where's Jason?"

"He's out front in his Dad's pick-up truck. Why, where you so adamant about him bringing me here in it, and not his Car?"

"Why? I'll show you why, come with me."

Rachael leads Lucy toward the garage, goes to her Car parked in the driveway, reaches inside to activate the garage door, as it slowly rises to reveal Rachael's purple motor scooter with a large red bow on it. Lucy covers her mouth so as to muffle a scream of utter delight, as Rachael announces,

"Happy Birthday, Lucy!"

"So that's why you wanted Jason to come here with me in his Dad's truck."

"Da, yeah, so you could take it home with you."

"That's awesome, but how do we get it up in the truck?"

"Lucy, my sweet unobservant friend, look to the bottom of the wall beside the scooter, you'll see a ramp, to do just that, I believe it was my Dad's, to get his Harley up into his truck."

As Lucy passes by Rachael on the driveway to go tell Jason, she stops to give her a big thank you hug saying,

"Thank you so much for this, this is the most fetch gift, and you are, the most excellent friend I will ever have! I Love you!"

"Love you too, Luc, now let's get the scooter on the truck so you can get it home, and come back to get me so we can go to the Mystic Pizza Restaurant to celebrate your Birthday."

Rachael drives the scooter to the end of the driveway where Jason's truck is parked, while Jason retrieves the ramp from the garage. They get it up inside the truck, secure it, and Rachael gives the keys and the two helmets to Lucy. As they drive away Lucy proclaims,

"We'll be back for you soon!"

Rachael turns on her heels, and heads to the back door to go in and get refreshed for the Celebration, stops to see that the food she had laid out as bait has been taken, and softly utters under her breath,

"Damn!"

Rachael goes up to her Bedroom to change her clothes, for the Gazebo roof has soiled the blouse she is wearing, and then refreshes her makeup. With these things done, she goes down to the Library office to review her Manuscript that she hasn't done any writing of in awhile, as she finishes reading what she has written, Jason and Lucy pull up in front of the house and sound the Car Horn. She grabs her jacket and heads out to the Car. Entering the Car Jason states,

"It's just too bad Shane's not here to go with us."

"Mmmm," she evasively answers him and thinks,

He's never around on the weekends, a good thing for him, but not for me, I'll need to make some changes somehow.

Jason continues,

"Rach, how long have you and Shane been together for?"

She doesn't answer right away, so Jason tries again.

"Rachael, Shane and you have been together for how long?"

She still doesn't answer, she's too deep in her private thoughts about her strange way of life, and having a relationship with someone that doesn't know, and may never be able to accept it.

So Lucy tries to get her attention,

"Rach, Rachael, Jason is asking you something."

With this she comes out of her thoughtful haze and answers,

"Yes, I would like pepperoni on my Pizza!"

"That's not what he asked you about." Lucy states, and then turns to Jason and says, "Jason ask her again."

"No, that's fine; I don't really need to know. Let's just have a fun night. Okay?"

"Sounds like a plan!"

Rachael agrees,

Lucy excitedly interjects,

"Yeah, a really fab Birthday plan!"

Chapter Seventeen

RACHAEL, AND CARMELLA, sit in the Library conversing about, the whys and wherefores of life, when they both hear a Vehicle pull in the driveway, and a door close.

Mella inquires,

"Rachael are you expecting someone?"

"Yes, Me-ma that should be Shane."

"Is this the Man in your life, that I have not met as of yet?"

"Yes, it is, I told you about him, you met him at my party."

"You mean the D.J., which did the music?"

"Yeah and please be nice to him Me-ma, I really like him a lot, and if I can be so bold, I believe I'm in Love with him."

"Your first real Love, my Dear?"

"I guess, I would say so."

"Well, that's wonderful, Sweetheart! But you sound unsure." I can't wait to sit and talk with him."

"Yeah I know, please be nice."

"Oh, I will."

At that moment Shane enters the room and says,

"Sorry Rachael, I'm a little late getting back, hit a lot of traffic on my way here."

Rachael makes the formal introduction,

"Carmella Valli, this is Shane, Shane Smith."

"So this is your Me-ma, I've heard so much about, it's nice to finally meet you formally, I know we met at the party, but I did not have time to talk and get to know you."

"Well, we have some time now."

Rachael interrupts,

"Me-ma, can I freshen your Coffee, and Shane would you like a cup?"

"Yes, my Dear, I would Love that."

Mella answers,

And Shane replies,

"I'd Love a cup, hun."

Rachael rises and collects her cup and Mella's, and begins to leave the room, she pauses to glance back at Mella with a firm look that imposes, please don't be too rough on him.

Mella looks Shane dead in his eyes and says,

"So I see you are staying here with my Granddaughter,

And what, may I ask, are your intentions toward her?"

"Well, Ma'am, I reckon I'd have to say, I have strong feelings for your Granddaughter."

"Would you say, strong enough to marry her?"

Before he can answer her, Rachael arrives with a tray of the Coffee and some cake too, announcing abruptly,

"Well, here we are, some fresh Coffee, and I thought we might have a little cake to go with it!"

Shane breathes a sigh of relief and says,

"That sounds great, and I would welcome a little something to eat after my long ride here."

They sit and enjoy the refreshments with a bit of small talk, as Shane tells, what Rachael already knows about him, but Mella did not, how he came to be here from Georgia to be living and working in this part of the country. After he finishes, Mella notices the time, and announces,

"Well, my Dears, it's getting late, I really should get going. I do have a bit of a ride home. It's been a pleasure to have met and talked with you, Shane. I hope you and Rach will come by my house soon, to get to meet her Grandfather, Michael, Sr."

With that, Shane rises and response, by taking her hand and saying,

"The pleasure was, all mine Mrs. Valli, I'm sure, and may I express my deepest sympathy for the loss of your son."

"Thank you, I really need to be on my way now."

Rachael and Mella embrace with a mutual kiss on each others cheek. Shane the gentleman that he is escorts Carmella, to her Car and sees her off.

After Mella has left, and Shane returns to the house, Rachael addresses him hardheartedly with;

"I was expecting you back this morning. Do I want to know what kept you late? And don't give me that heavy traffic reason again, it's beginning to get lame."

"Rachael, what's that suppose ta mean?"

Rachael hesitates for a moment before answering him, and thinks,

I have to make this sound like it really bothers me, to the point of creating a rift in our relationship, in the attempt to have us break up, and get him out of my life, so he'll be safe from me and what I could do to him. Losing him would be harder for me than him, but he will never know it.

Shane stands patiently waiting for her to answer him.

She bows her head and begins,

"Shane I know what it's like for a D.J., working in popular Dance Clubs in the Big Apple, not to mention private functions you do, all the women what your attention, and I'd have to assume sometimes more than that."

"Rachael, please, I'm in Love with you. Why would I give in to one of them?"

"Why is not important, would, is the problem I have, sitting here without you, while they have you!"

"Have **me**! They don't have **me**!"

"They have more, of you than I do!"

"Rach, you're being silly!"

"Silly. **Silly**. I'm being silly?

"Wait, I mean, you're…

Rachael cuts him off, and fires back at him angrily,

"If you think that I'm just a silly, stupid little Girl like one of your Club D.J. groupies, you can go sleep in your van from now on!"

"Rachael, now you're being foolish!"

She gets even more agitated,

"Oh, so now I'm foolish! Foolish! Get what you need and get **OUT**!

"Rachael, please listen!"

"No! You listen; I said get out, **NOW**! Just go, and don't look back!"

"Okay! I'll go! But this doesn't mean I don't Love you."

As Shane makes his way up the Grand Staircase to get his things, Rachael has some emotional thoughts,

What it does mean, my Love, is that I Love you so much, that I want you to be safe from my ***Blood Passion****, so we must part, but you will never know the real reason, but you will be alive, because if I were to ever harm, or kill you, I wouldn't,* ***no****, I couldn't live with that.*

Shane comes slowly down the stairs, with his packed rucksack over his shoulder and heads for the front door, opens it, and before continuing, he stops, turns round to where Rachael is sitting on the couch in the Living Room, for one last appeal to her, but before he can utter a word, she declares as she looks up and over to him,

"Just go!"

No words of goodbye are exchanged, she just hears the door click closed and breathes a sigh of relief, knowing that it's over, and he'll be safe.

Wiping a single tear from her cheek, having some final thoughts on the subject of Love in her life,

Will I ever be able to have an enduring Love in my life, or am I destined to be alone until this… my extraordinary existence is over?

Oh, Father, I feel ever closer to you, now.

Chapter Eighteen

RACHAEL RISES SLOWLY from the couch, enters the Library, walks over to the front windows, hears the door of Shane's Company van close and watches as he backs out of the driveway to make his way down Cedar Lane.

Turning round, wipes another tear from her cheek, and walks over to the Desk to finally get back to her writing of her Manuscript, to hopefully take her mind off of what just happened.

Rachael reviews what has been written, and starts writing from where she had left off;

Mia sits at her Kitchen table with her head bowed down, with her elbows on the table, her forehead rests in the palms of her hands, trying to gather her thoughts an make sense of all of it. At the same time Marcus arrives back in the park to the scene of the incident, to find Lucas is nowhere in sight, and suddenly he has an awfully disturbing thought,

'Lucas may have seen me leaving, with Mia in my arms, and followed us. I must get back to Mia's place, ***now****, to see that she is there, and that she's all right.'*

With Mia's safety now his top priority, he bolts back to Mia's Beacon Hill apartment building, where he rings her bell, but gets no immediate response, he waits impatiently in the small foyer, leaning up against the wall tapping his foot nervously.

After a few seemingly long agonizing moments, he exits the building, and walks backward across her street, to get a look up at her apartment windows to see that the lights are on, feeling vaguely relieved, he looks round to see if anyone is about, not seeing anyone he brings out his Vampyre attributes of heightened hearing, attempting to hear any sounds coming from her place, he gains no evidence of her presents in her apartment this way, so he decides to get up to her windows by using his Vampyre powers of scaling the wall, to get a look inside, and possibly gain entrance. He peers in, looks round of what he can see of the apartment finding all looks quiet.

Poised now at the window he continues his vigil for a few more seconds, he sees no movement inside, but he can't see the Kitchen from his vantage point, so he pushes the window up, and it opens, so he quietly climbs inside, unfortunately knocking over a lamp that crashes to the floor with a loud bang; he freezes for a moment to await someone, hopefully Mia, being alerted to his presents. But no one comes, he stands, and walks stealthfully to the Kitchen to discover that no ones there, but one of the chairs is knocked over and the table is slightly askew, it seems to him that a struggle has taken place, he calls out softly,

"Mia? Mia are you here?"

Suddenly the Kitchen back door bursts open, as Mia sees Marcus, quickly closing the space between them, throws her arms around him, and proclaims with uneasy breathing,

"Marcus! I'm so glad to see ***you****!"*

"The feeling is mutual, I assure you. What happened ***here****?"*

"Well, okay, let me see," She begins after sitting down, "I hadn't noticed right away that a small window on the back door was broken, allowing someone to gain entrance, until while I was sitting at the table with my back to the door, lost in my thoughts, I was accosted from behind by my mouth being covered by someone's gloved hand, I struggled to look up and back, to see Lucas, our attacker. He then picked me up and forced me with him out the door, as he started to coerce me down the back stairs, I believe he misplaced his footing and lost his grip on me, this afforded me the chance I needed to push him away and down the stairs, and here I am!"

"Marcus, how did he know where I live?"

As Marcus turns round from checking the back Staircase he answers her,

"Lucas, is what we call in the Cabal, a hunter, tracker, he has some extraordinary abilities for finding people, to say the least. And you my Dear, have now witnessed this tonight twice; first in the park, and now at your apartment."

"What will you do, now?"

"What I will do is; ask you to gather up some of your clothing and anything else you feel you need for a few days, because you are coming with me, to meet with the Cabal and face Quintus and get this settled, one way or another. Leaving you here, I'm afraid, is not an option for your safety. Lucas, most likely will try again to kidnap you to be used as bait, to get me to face the Cabal, so we'll need to cut him to the quick, beat him to the punch, as it were, in order to keep you from any harm. I'm so sorry, to get you involved in all this, because if any harm should befall you, I'd never be able to forgive myself."

As Mia goes about quickly gathering up what's needed, she has a thought,

'Keep me from harm, I'd say that means he does care about me.'

Marcus takes another look outback, to find to his delight, no signs of Lucas, he calls out to Mia from the Kitchen,

"Mia, please, make it fast, we must be going, it's at least a forty five minute ride to Mystic, Connecticut, where the Cabal is clandestinely based."

"I'll be ready in a moment, and we can get going!"

At that exact moment, Rachael's Cell-phone resting on the Desk, rings. She looks to see; who it is that's calling, to find that it's her Mother, not in any mood to talk with anyone, so lets it go to voice mail.

After driving all night, and getting a small amount of sleep on the office couch, it is now being morning, Shane walks into a frequented Coffee Shop. He buys a cup at the counter and goes to sit down at a table, unfortunately finding that all the tables are occupied, he approaches one with a Woman with auburn hair sitting alone, with her head down reading something that appears to be a Medical Text Book, he stands at her table and greets her with,

"Excuse me, Miss. May I sit a spell to have my Coffee?"

Looking up at him, they both are taken aback by what they see, declaring simultaneously, each others name;

She proclaims,

"Shane!"

He counters,

"Cheryl!"

As he slowly pulls out the chair to sit down, he questions her,

"What brings **you** here, to the Big Apple?"

"Work!"

"I thought you didn't want to leave the Atlanta Medical Center in Georgia to come with me to New York City. What changed your mind?"

"Like I said, work!"

Shane questionably reiterates,

"Work?"

"Yeah, not long after you left, they were starting staff layoffs at the Medical Center, so I put in for a transfer to a Hospital up here, and yes, I have, missed you a little."

"I don't understand why you didn't call me, to let me know."

"I did, but your phone was turned off, so I tried the 'MusicSmith' office, and left a few messages, but after you didn't respond I gave up. Surmising you didn't want to have any contact with me."

"No, Cheryl, you've got it wrong, my cousin gave me a company Cell-phone so I shut down my own. And the Girl my cousin has in the office, is a real ditz! I never got your messages."

"Well, Shane, how have you been?"

He looks down into his Coffee cup and responds vaguely,

"Long story… busy with work."

"You'll have ta tell me all about it, sometime soon."

"Soon? Sounds like you'd like to hear it."

"Perhaps I would, I am free for dinner tonight!"

Shane has a hopeful thought,

Feels like my ex Cheryl May, is just the medicine I'll need to get pass, what just happened to me, Cheryl was always a life saver.

"Kool Beans! Where, and what time should I come to collect you?"

Cheryl, takes out a small notepad from her bag, writes down her address, holds it out to him smiling and adds,

"Eight o'clock will be suitable!"

Shane has his trademark gratifying expression in his mind,

Kool Beans!

As he obtains the note from her hand, he replies as he gets up to leave,

"Right then! See you, tonight!"

Chapter Nineteen

RACHAEL RISES SLOWLY from the Desk chair, and begins to pace the floor, her Cell-phone rings again, making her way back to stand at the Desk with the chair behind her, picks up the phone to see who it is that's calling now. It turns out to be Lucy this time, reluctantly answering it,

"What up Lucy?"

"Jason, and I, would like to get together with Shane and you, to do something fun this coming weekend. What do you say?"

"Sorry, Lucy, but that would be impossible!"

"Impossible! Why, because, Shane will be working in New York City?"

Rachael replies with a tone of sadness in her voice,

"No, Lucy, that's not it, Shane, and I are no longer together."

'What! Why?"

Rachael, getting a bit irritable answers,

"Lucy what are you four years old? With all the whys?"

"But, Rach, you guys were, so I thought, really in Love. What in the world happened?"

"Well, in my world, it turned out not to be so."

"Not to be so! Why?"

"Why, again! Lucy I have to go, talk later!"

With that, she hangs up abruptly.

She places the phone down, hoping to get back to her writing. But to her frustration, her phone rings once more, this time, it's her Mother calling again. Before answering it, she has a quick thought,

Should have turned the darn thing off, or I'll never finish my novel.

Reluctantly, answers it with,

"Hi Mom."

"Rachael, Dear, are you busy this coming weekend? We were hoping that, Shane and you would like to come by for a Barbecue on Saturday."

"Mom, I'm sure we'd like to, but Shane will be in New York City working."

"Oh, that's right, I'm sorry I forgot he works most weekends. Well then how about you come by, and you could bring Lucy and whomever else you like with you, there'll be plenty of food!"

Rachael now thinks,

Time to do something; I never liked to do, especially to my Mother. Lie!

"Sorry Mom, already have plans. Some other time, perhaps?"

"Sure, my Dear, I'll give you a rain check!"

"Thanks Mom. Love you guys, bye!"

"Love you too, bye."

Rachael slams down her phone on the Desk and says out loud,

"Shane and you! Shane and you! How long will I be hearing people saying that to me?"

"I don't really need a **Blood Passion** feeding this coming weekend, but I'd like to have one just the same."

She brings out her Father's Memoirs from the top drawer of the Desk, to go over it one more time of how and where her Father went in Hartford to do his feedings. With his instructions now fresh in her mind, she stands up and leans in and slams down both her hands on the Desk, and proclaims adamantly,

"If, I can't have **Love**, then **I will have Blood**!"

Completing her statement with an assertive thought,

*Whenever I **want** it, not just when I **need** it!*

The next few days go by without incident, except for a small article in a local weekly newspaper that is regularly delivered to her house. Perusing through this Mystic Tabloid, she comes across a sort of curious, but grotesque article on page four, taking notice of it for the simple reason; that there is an ad near it for the business Shane works for, 'MusicSmith'. The article is somewhat of a disturbing nature, a short piece about an unidentified young Mans' body that washed up on a Newport Beach in Rhode Island. It goes on to say, that the authorities would have a difficult job of identifying this person, because it's been decapitated, and the hands are also missing, and there are no identifying items like a wallet or any distinguishing marks on the body that they can use; the Medical Examiner claims it has been in the water for some time and that some sharks probably got at it, hence the mutilations. A note is added at the end, in bold lettering as follows; if anyone knows of a young male missing person within the last six months or so, in the general area, please contact the Rhode Island Police. That is all it was to the story. Rachael crumbles it up, throws it away, without giving it a second thought.

During the course of the week, in between her household tasks, and running a few errands to downtown Mystic, she makes the attempt, a few times, to get back to her writing, but can't come up with any good ideas of where to take the story from where it leaves off, slight case of Writer's Block, perhaps, feeling and believing that a fresh **Blood Passion** feeding may help stimulate her imagination.

So it's now being Saturday evening, she'll venture out to Hartford at about nine, and see what she will find, not really needing a feeding, she can take her time, and maybe have herself a little fun with it.

At about eight thirty, she prepares herself for the ride, by wearing all black clothing, and not having anything that could identify her. She goes into the garage by its side door, gets in the Car, opens the electronic overhead door, pulls out onto the driveway, stops to put the top down, taking note that it's a Bella

Luna night, which means there is a large bright full moon shining down on her. She precisely follows what her Father had done, and finds herself at the same location; walking the streets of Hartford for a while, getting a feel for the surroundings, but not making any eye contact with anyone. Eventually coming to the location of the walkway that's between two large buildings, that her Father had mentioned, and been to himself, like it says in his Memoir, stopping only to gradually open the unlocked gate, and enter, walking the length of it slowly, until getting to the far end of it where it meets a back street, where she has a look around, casing the area, seeing that no one is about, and then brings out her full Vampire attributes and then turns round, to leisurely walk back in the direction she came. In this way, with her Vampire powers, of her heighten senses of sight, and smell alerts her that there's someone sitting on the ground near a large barrel, they weren't there just a second ago, stopping a few feet away from the barrel, seeing now with her night vision that it's a lone Man, drinking from a bottle inside a plain brown paper bag, she then gradually approaches where he is sitting, stops, and so he wouldn't see her face, not looking down at him. This person assumes, that it's a young Female; he then lowers the bottle from his mouth to look up at her, and claims in a slurred somewhat concerned manner,

"Hey, young lady don't you know that it could be dangerous for a young Girl to be here in a dark alley all alone."

She turns her head to look down at him, then bends down to grab him by his clothing, swiftly bringing him up to be face to face with her, and announces harshly,

"Oh, yeah, more for you, then for me, I would think, here I'll show you why."

With that said and this derelict, being stunned by what he sees, she quickly takes hold of his hair, pulling his head back to get a clear means to his neck, opening her salivating mouth and plunging her long fangs into his neck until fulfilled with his Blood.

Rachael lets go of the now empty vessel, for it to fall back to where it was, gives herself a moment to take pleasure in the feeling of power, and fulfillment throughout her body, shifts her clothing and with her gloved hand wipes any Blood from around her mouth, and composedly walks out to the street, making her way to her Car parked not too far away, gets in and caringly takes her leave of Hartford, with a wicked thought in her mind,

Thanks for the memories!

Now driving down the highway toward home, having some further thoughts;

Perhaps, I should give the Vampire side of me its own name, similar to what my Dad had given to his. Okay, let me see, ah… how about something kind of like a feminine form of the name Malice, like; Malevolence, with the Surname; Nightwing, again like my Father had done. Yeah! I like it, ***no****, I Love it! That will do for me, just fine, so declaring out loud just to hear the sound of it;*

"Malevolence Nightwing; Child of Malice!"

She then bears down hard on the gas pedal, purposely increasing her speed to get herself home quicker.

Chapter Twenty

ARRIVING BACK IN Mystic, Rachael cruises Main Street, to see if anyone that she knows is around, being too keyed up to go home right now. Not seeing anyone she knows that's usually hanging outside of the Mystic Pizza Restaurant, so she drives on to the east side of Town, to check out the lounge at the Ebb Tide Restaurant, as she enters, catching sight of Lucy, and Jason at a table just off to her left, at the same time Lucy sees her and calls out,

"Hey Rach, what up?"

"Lucy, Jason, nice to see you guys. What's the word?"

"The word is, as you put it, Happy Birthday to Jason, he's twenty two today!"

"That's so boss, Jace. What's Lucy giving you for your Birthday? Or has she already given it to you?"

Lucy looks up at Rachael, and shyly remarks,

"Why, whatever do you mean?"

"Oh, I don't know what do you think, I mean?"

Jason stands up, pulls out a chair for Rachael as he breaks into the conversation,

"Rach, please join us, can I get you something from the bar?"

"Yeah, that would be nice, a glass of red Wine, and tell Nick it's for me."

Before he can leave to go to the bar, their waitress, Beth comes to their table to ask,

"May I get anyone a refill?"

"Yeah, we'll have another round, and you can bring Rachael here, a glass of red Wine."

Jason replies.

"Hey, Lucy, I didn't notice Jason's Car in the parking lot."

"Yeah, well, we knew we'd be drinking, so just like you and I did when we came here to celebrate your twenty first, we took a Cab."

Rachael roguishly inquires, scanning the room,

"Hey, any hot guys here tonight?"

Lucy replies,

"Sorry, Rach haven't noticed, I've been too busy with my hot Birthday Boy!"

As Beth, returns with the drink order, Jason stands to excuse himself to use the Men's Room.

With him gone for the moment, Rachael leans in close to Lucy to pose an intimate and somewhat personal query,

"So did you two get busy or what?"

Lucy answers her a bit offended,

"Rach, please, that's a little intrusive, don't you think?"

"Intrusive! Come on Lucy you're a big Girl. And how long have we known each other? My Lord, it's been like forever now, I think we can be open with each other about these things."

"Well, if we can be that open, I'll tell you that, I'm thinking of getting a room at the Ebb Tide Motel for the night. But I'm really not sure how to go about it."

"Let me handle it for you, it can be my Birthday present for you both!"

Rachael gets up and says,

"Give me a minute, I'll be right back."

Lucy interjects,

"Rachael!"

"Lucy, please, you'll thank me in the morning!"

Jason arrives back to the table, sits down and asks,

"Hey, Lucy, where'd Rachael get to?"

"Oh, she'll be right back; gone to get something for your Birthday!"

"Something for my Birthday! At this time of night? What does she have, something in her Car?"

"Not exactly!"

Rachael comes back and abruptly stops at the table, picks up her Wine, drops the room key on the table saying,

"Here you go, you guys have a real fab night, and I'll just go tell Nick to put all your drinks on my tab, and have him send something nice to your room, now get yourselves out of here before I change my mind!"

They get up to hastily leave, concurrently saying,

"Thanks Rach!"

"Not another word, now go! Lucy we'll talk soon!"

Rachael makes her way to the bar to tell Nick to charge all their drinks to her tab, and send a bottle of bubbly and two glasses to room twenty two at the Ebb Tide Motel.

Nick agrees, saying,

"No problem, Rach that was so sweet, what you did for them."

"Oh, you saw that. Did you?"

"Nick, don't miss much in this place."

So Rachael finishes her Wine and beginning to feel a bit fatigued, gives Nick a healthy tip, says good night to him, and takes her leave of the lounge

Arrives home about fifteen minutes later, enters through the back door into the Kitchen, drops her keys on the table, loudly announcing,

"Honey! I'm home! Oh, wait, there's no one here!"

Suddenly, from nowhere, a somewhat haunting familiar voice declares,

"I wouldn't say that!"

"Hey, so you are back! Where've you been? I am kind of glad you have returned, because I think I know who you are, or should

I say were, it's now time you, and I, have a little heart to heart, if you even have one that is."

"I do remember actually having one, at one time, that is."

"That is, when you were actually alive?"

"Oh, smart Girl! And just who do you think that I was?"

"Oh, that was sort of easy to figure out, really!"

"Well, are you going to tell me who you presumed that I was, or what?"

"Yeah, just let me get myself a glass of Wine and sit before I continue, knowing what you are, I'm totally aware that time has no meaning for you."

"Okay, Rachael, so you now have your Wine, and are seated, now, let me hear who you say that you think I am, or was!"

"Not think. I know! It was fairly easy to work out, let me see, the night you came to help me seduce Shane, it sounded to me that you were rather a loose Woman at one time in your life, very experienced in the art of the seduction of the Male, so that would eliminate my late Great Grandmother, most women of her generation weren't in the practice of doing such things, unless they were shall I say, women of the night!"

"Are you saying...

Rachael cuts her off with,

"Not at all **Marlena**, my Dear now departed, endearing Godmother that endeavored to kill me and my Mother!"

With Rachael's statement of recognition, of who this really is,

Marlena having now been found out, her ethereal image slowly starts to materialize, proclaiming,

"Oh, that! Well, I only tried to kill you guys a little! After all it was kill, or be killed."

"Cute! How does one kill someone a little? Oh, never mind, it's a rhetorical question. So tell me, my Dear Godmother, what is it you want with me?"

"I'll tell you, but you probably won't believe me, anyway."

Chapter Twenty-One

RACHAEL SITS WAITING for Marlena, to continue with what she has to say, sipping her Wine and thinks,

Okay, so she's now haunting my house, did she witness what I did to her son James, or what; somehow I will have to find out without asking her about it directly.

As Rachael continues to think, Marlena finally begins to say what she had begun to,

"My Dear Godchild, for me to be able to get to my final resting place, and to be once again united with my belated loved ones; my husband, James, Sr. and my Daughter, Gabrielle, I must first help you, as much as I can, to deal with your anomalous way of living."

"Okay, why would I not, believe you, after all, didn't my Dad do the same thing with you, and me?"

"Yes, come to think of it, I think you're right about that!"

Rachael has a quick thought,

Well, I guess she doesn't know about James yet, and by the time she does find out she'll be with him, her Husband, and her Daughter, and I would believe she won't be able to come back here, to trouble me any more.

"Well, my Dear Godmother that will be nice I suppose."

"You suppose! Why you little whit…"

"Now now, Marlena temper, temper! This is no time for a hizzey fit! And just how do you presume you can help me?"

"Well, let me see, you just lost, or should I say, sent away for his own safety, and may I dare add, he will never know the actual reason why, the Man who was your first Love, and your first sexual encounter!"

"In which you did help me with that, little alluring deed!"

"Yes, my Dear, and I do believe you enjoyed it. Did you not?"

"Yeah Yeah, no need to go into the details, so you were watching, you said I was on my own after your last encouraging statement in the hall outside of Shane's Bedroom. Right?"

"Yeah, well, yes, I did, but I just had to take a little peek for myself. After all, I was the initiator of your first sexual encounter, and I myself can't do that sort of thing anymore and I did, so much, enjoy it, in my life."

"Oh, that's lovely, my Godmother watched me have sex for the first time in my life!"

"Now now Rachael, who's having the hizzey fit, now?"

"Yeah, well, I just feel a little uncomfortable about it. By the way, how did I do?"

"You did just fine; it was your first time and all!"

"Well, now that that's cleared up. How can you, help me out with having any kind of Love in my life?"

"Ah, let me see, first you will need to find someone that Loves you enough to want to be like you."

"Like me?"

"Yes, like you, having a need to ingest Human Blood on a regular basis."

"I didn't need that reminder of want I need to, do to survive. Do you really think that I could find someone like that?"

"Maybe not around here, but like in that little Manuscript you are writing, which by the way, isn't half bad, in any large metropolis like New York City perhaps."

"Are you suggesting that I move?"

"You may not have a choice on that, going round, leaving dead bodies absent of their Blood, it could catch up with you, sooner or later."

"You were never caught, were you?"

"I did have a close call one night in Providence."

"That must have been awful!"

"Not really, the Police are not as smart as they lead us to believe. Getting away from them was close, yes, but with the powers that I did possess it was quite easy, really!"

"Powers? What kind of powers did you have?"

"I know you've read your Father's Memoirs. He tells of what they were in there. You have some of them; I've witnessed first hand a few of yours."

"Yes, read it many times, it also tells of how to go about turning someone, like he was going to try on my Mother. But at the last minute changes her mind, which led to the end of his reign as Malice Nightwing, The First."

"That's history, my Dear, distressing history!"

"Do you think a turning would work the way he describes it?"

"That my sweet, would depend."

"Marlena stop talking in riddles. Depends on what?"

"Oh, on whether, or not your partner is willing to go through with it, I would imagine. Like he wrote it's never been documented as really happening, so it would be a shot in the dark, I would think."

Marlena continues with a question,

"My Dear, do you have the voice in your head like me and your Father had?"

"No, thank God! I inherited my condition from birth, not from some mysterious Mutated Vampire Bat biting me!"

"Well, in that you are lucky! It made me crazy, nuts, and do things I really didn't want to, at times!"

"Yeah, my Mom and I witnessed that, for sure, like the time…!"

"Rachael, please, no need to elaborate on those times, I do still remember them!"

So, not to change the subject, but what's it like to be… dead?"

"Hard to explain really, a feeling of total freedom, at first, but then it's kind of a bummer that you can't interact with a solid object in the living world, your Dad, I believe was able, but I never had him tell me how he could do it. Did he tell you how he could, when you made contact with him the night you broke into this house when it was mine?"

"No, he did not, we didn't have a lot of time together, and I had to get out before you came back, and found me here."

"That's okay, if he could make it happen, then so can I!"

"Marlena, that's super, you go work on that, while I get back to my little Manuscript, we can continue this another time, because I believe, I just came up with a good idea for my story. So talk later?"

"Yeah later."

And with that, Marlena dissipates back up into the Attic, while Rachael takes her Wine, heads to the Library to possibly get back to her writing, then realizing that she could use some sleep first, so once again her novel gets delayed.

Chapter Twenty-Two

RACHAEL WAKES ABOUT eight hours later, goes in her sleeping attire, with a fresh glass of Wine to her Desk in the Library, sits herself down in front of her Laptop opens it, and brings up her Manuscript. She sits back in her chair, to review in her thoughts, of what she had envisioned, while in her conversation with the spirit of Marlena last night, of writing, to continue her story of The Mystic Vampyres.

Just as she begins to type she hears from outside, the familiar sound of a Scooter pulling into her driveway, it stops, and the engine shuts off, then she hears the unmistakable voice of Lucy, loudly calling out her name,

"**RACHAEL**!"

With a huff, she rises, closes the Computer, and makes her way out of the room hears Lucy loudly knocking at the back door. She calls out loudly,

"All right all right, hold your horses Lucy, I'm coming!"

Having the thought of,

Like I said before, at this rate, I'll never get my book done.

Arriving at the door, opening it, Lucy bursts in saying,

"Rach, oh Bestie, we really need to talk!"

Another thought immediately enters Rachael's mind,

Why does everyone, need to talk with me?

Lucy continues as she goes to the Fridge to get a soda,

"Rach, please sit, and talk to me!"

"Yeah yeah, Lucy you're acting like your jeans are on fire!"

"What's that, ta mean?"

"Oh, Lucy it's a joke! What is it you want to talk about?"

"First, I want to say, thank you so much for Jason's Birthday night gift, I mean thing, I mean gift! Oh, I'm not sure what I mean, but thanks from me, and Jason anyway."

"Okay, but it's not really necessary, I felt it would go without saying, but you both are welcome! And what is the second thing on your mind?"

"Well," She dipped her head and continues, "The thing you had told me to always have with me in my bag, came in handy for what we did."

"So! You guys did **it**?"

Keeping her head down Lucy answers,

"Yeah, we did **it**!"

"Good for you two, now my turn. Been meaning to ask you what it was, the night of the party, that you were doing going out to the wooded area of my Backyard."

Lucy jerks her head up, takes a long swallow of her soda, places it down on the table and says,

"You want to know what I was doing, going…."

Rachael cuts her off,

"Don't even think of telling me a lie, I was attacked by something that almost got you! So, only the truth will do, Bestie!"

"Yeah, the truth. Okay, the truth, Jason wanted me to meet him out there to…"

Rachael cuts her off again,

"To **what**, do **it**? Do **it**, in my yard?"

"**No**, Rach, he said he just wanted to make out with me a little, where no one could see us."

"Men! I mean Boys, what is it with them?"

"Well, Rach, I think…"

Once again Rachael cuts her off,

"Lucy, don't even try to answer that, it's a rhetorical question. Okay now, Lucy go on with your answer."

"Oh yeah, well, while I was waiting for him to show, I saw what looked like two small red eye thingies coming at me, but rather low to the ground, and I froze, that's when I called out to you!"

"Good thing for you, there was a lull in the music, so I could hear you call to me."

"But not so good for you, I'm truly sorry!"

"That's fine, I mean what are Besties for?"

Lucy looks at Rachael, with a big smile and proclaims,

"For being Besties forever! Right? Wait, Rachael you just said that you were attacked, I heard you say the night of the party that you had tripped and fell, and that is how you hurt your arm. Why would you lie like that?"

"It was a tiny fib, I didn't want to start a panic and spoil the party. I did fall, evading my attacker, I tripped on something, and after all it was pretty dark out there, I was hurt in the fall, so it was close to the truth, just didn't mention the part about being attacked!"

"But… but your arm is okay now? Right?"

"Yes, Lucy don't give it another thought, it's fine."

"Rach, what was it that attacked you?"

"It was too dark to tell, Lucy just let it go, please."

"Okay, if you're all right, I will."

With that said, they both rise from the table, hug and Lucy takes her leave of the Cliff House. As Lucy exits Rachael says,

"Remember Lucy, do be careful driving that Scooter!"

"Yes, I will! Just like you taught me to!"

Rachael turns on her heels and heads back to the Library, with a happy thought,

Now to get back to my writing!

Just before entering the Library, hearing Lucy start up the Scooter, and begin to leave the driveway and then hears her suddenly stop and loudly declare,

"Oh, Hello, Mrs. DeClerico, Rachael's inside I'm just leaving, bye."

"Bye Dear, please be careful on that thing!"

Lucy hollers back, as while slowly making her way down Cedar Lane,

"**I will**!"

Inside the house, Rachael stops at the Library archway and has a questioning thought,

O great! Mom's here, what ever could she be wanting? I'll never get my novel finished, under these conditions. Maybe, like Marlena said I need to move or just get away somewhere until I've completed it.

The Doorbell chimes, Rachael knowing who it is, proclaims loudly,

"I'm coming Mom!"

Opening the door, Mina bursts in questioningly asking,

"Rachael, we haven't seen you at Elm Place for weeks, is there some reason you're avoiding your family? And have you seen that dreadful article in the Mystic News, about a young Man's body washing up on a beach in Newport, Rhode Island, a while ago?"

"Mom, please chill, I'm not avoiding my family, just been a little busy is all, and yes I did see the article. And yeah so, what of **it**? You don't think…"

"What of **it**! A person is, **dead**, Rachael! I never thought, in my wildest dreams, I'd be asking my Daughter something like this, but did you have anything to do with **it**?"

Mina sits in one of the chairs in the front sitting room to calm herself down, takes in a deep breath, looking up at Rachael with a sympathetic expression and inquires,

"Oh Dear, my Dear sweet child… have you started feeding on Human Blood yet? And don't even try to lie to me, because I'll know if you are!"

Chapter Twenty-Three

"MOTHER, YOU KNOW that I can't lie to you about something like this, but I also can't tell you the truth about it, either."

"What on earth do you mean, Rachael? That you can't or you won't, tell me the truth about it, either you had something to do with it, or you didn't!"

Rachael sits down in the chair next to Mina, gently taking her Mother's hand in hers, replying,

"It's not quite that simple, Mom! First of all, they haven't or they can't identify this Man's body!"

"What are you saying? That you've killed more then one young Man, so you don't know which one it could be?"

"No, I'm not saying that at all!"

"Dear God, Rachael how many have you killed?"

"At this house. Two!"

"Too, like in too many to say?

"No! It's the number two."

"And elsewhere, how many? Tell me, since it's been weeks since I've seen or heard from you, surely there must be more! Please do not tell me that one of them was… Shane!"

"No Mother! One of them was not Shane, we had a quarrel and he left, he's back in New York City, I would imagine, please Mom, do we have to get into this right now?"

"My one and only Daughter is going round murdering people, so I'd say yes we do!"

"Why, what do you think you can do to stop this… this, my way of existing with my condition?"

Mina pulls her hand away and stands up, now looking down at Rachael, and says,

"Condition! You've always called it your condition! I can't do much about your condition as you call it… I mean, this way you are living, but I do feel somewhat responsible for it in my own way! My god Rachael, you are taking lives!"

Mina looks down at the floor, and has a quick thought,

The awful nightmare I had a little before Rachael was born, about giving birth to a monster is now becoming a reality. Dear Lord, please forgive me for being so imprudent, maybe I will have to do something to stop her, but what?

Rachael attempts to break into her Mother's thought filled mental absence,

"Mom! Mother? Mom, answer me!"

Mina comes out from her reflection with,

"Yes, Rachael, my child, I'm here. By the way, what time is it?"

Rachael looks up at the Grandfather clock behind Mina and replies,

"It's a little before noon. Why?"

"Oh Dear, I must leave now to go get your Brother, Mathew!"

With that said, Mina rushes out to her Car and speeds off.

As Rachael watches her drive away down Cedar Lane, softly saying to herself,

"By all means, Dear Mother, do get on with your life, don't let me stop **you**! And **you**… won't be stopping me!"

Backing her way into the house, Rachael has some atrocious questioning thoughts,

To what length, might she be willing to go to try to stop me? Would she turn me in to the authorities for them to attempt to destroy me? I mean, would my very own Mother do something like that to her own Daughter?

In her frustration repeats the questions aloud, hoping that Marlena can and will hear her,

"Would my own Mother do something like that to me? Would my own Mother turn me in to the authorities…? Well Marlena, could she? Would she? Will my very own Mother do something like that to her only Daughter?"

From an undetectable place in the room, Marlena's voice emanates,

"Rachael, sounds to me like you're getting a bit paranoid and you're asking the wrong person the wrong question, my Dear! Maybe, you might pose the question as, should she?"

"Paranoid? Aha, so it's a, coulda'… woulda'… shoulda' thing. Is it?"

"I, myself, wouldn't underestimate anyone, but that's just me, my Dear!"

"Yeah, well, maybe it's not just you; perhaps I should start thinking like you do!"

"Marlena! Marlena! Marlena? Are you…? She's gone; I hate it when she does that!"

As Rachael irritatedly paces the front sitting room floor, thinking,

I'm too keyed up now, to do any writing, maybe I'll just go for a ride.

Grabbing her sleeveless jacket from the back of the Kitchen chair and her keys off the Table, exits the back door, steps down the arching cement stairs to the brick path that leads to the side door of the garage, which exposes her to direct sunlight; begins to feel a warming sensation that quickly becomes a burning feeling on any of her exposed skin, quickly stepping back into the shaded area of the yard where the burning feeling disperses, sitting down on the back steps, in the shade, contemplating,

Oh, boy, I'm now not able to go out into the sunlight; seems like exposure to direct sunlight, is harmful to me, now? Possibly because I've had numerous ***Blood Passion*** *feedings, I'm now becoming more like my Dad was only being able to go outside, if I stay in the shade or on an overcast day or at night! Somewhat of a nocturnal creature, like my Father and Marlena were.*

She gets up from the stairs, makes her way back into the house, continuing to reflect,

I will now notify all, that I will need solitude, and little to no contact so as to finish writing my Manuscript, because like my Dad says in his Memoir it should be full speed ahead until it is done. If they can't understand, and comply with my wishes, then I might have to go away somewhere to be alone to finish it.

Now in the Library, at the Desk, she begins making phone calls, to all that would be concerned about her wellbeing, telling them, or leaving, to the ones that don't answer, a voice mail of her request for solitude for her writing, assuring them she'll be in touch when finished with it. Of the ones she speaks with they understand and wish her well.

Finished with this task, pours herself a new glass of Wine; leans back in her chair, and says,

"I believe another trip to downtown Hartford is in order, tonight."

The haunting voice of Marlena emanates in the room,

"Now that's the Spirit!"

"The Spirit! I'd guess **you'd** be the one to know all about that kind of thing!"

Rachael replies, than makes her way to the Living Room Couch, to get a cat nap to be refreshed for her trip to downtown Hartford, later this evening.

Chapter Twenty-Four

RACHAEL ENTERS HARTFORD in her usual method then makes her way to the alley that she frequently haunts, knowing that there will be pray to feed on. Entering it seeing that there is quite the group of deviants hanging about, lying low for a few minutes, and hiding in the shadows watching to see who stays and who goes. After a little while the group thins out, she brings on her Vampire Night Vision to see that, only two of them have stayed to share a bottle of something in a plain brown bag, with her enhanced hearing, able to hear them speak of one of their number who was recently found dead, with very little Blood left in its body. To be sure, Rachael knows what happened to this buddy of theirs.

They talk of the Police making inquiries in and around Hartford, but it seems like they are getting nowhere in their investigation of this bizarre occurrence. Rachael breathes a small sigh of relief, brings out her full Vampire attributes, and then begins stealthfully to move toward them. Quietly comes up behind one of them, swiftly wrapping her arm around its neck, with a force to choke and cut off, it's breathing, she bites into this first victim's neck, as the other lunges at her, with blind drunken boldness, only to be grabbed by Rachael's free hand, clutching its neck, but not in time to stop it from letting out a somewhat loud gurgling squeal, lifting up this alleged defender about a foot off the ground, to continue squeezing its throat so as to stop it from making another sound of any kind. Unfortunately for Rachael, the sound that it had let out was heard by some people, lingering on the Sidewalk at one end of the Alleyway. One person begins to go in the alley to investigate, but his companion quickly grabs him by the arm saying,

"What are you nuts, going in there? It's probably some drunks fighting over a bottle of Wine."

As he lets go of his friend's arm, a Police cruiser pulls up to the sidewalk to see what is happening with these two people. An officer exits the Car onto the sidewalk asking,

"What's the trouble here?"

"Oh, nothing Sir, we just heard a strange sound coming from the alley is all."

"Okay, you people, move along now, the Police will handle this!"

Rachael hears all that has, and is being said and, happening out on the sidewalk, quickly finishing her **Blood Passion** feeding, drops both deviants to the ground, starts to walk quickly to the other end of the alley to make her escape, after about twenty feet, she finds that a recently installed barrier blocks her path, standing still, thinking of what to do about her dilemma. As the Police draw closer to her location, she strains to remember something in her Dad's Memoir about having the power to be able to scale a sheer wall like a spider or something like it, but she does remember that there was no detailed instruction on how to go about it. She looks up at the wall of the building, and concentrates on accomplishing this task, what seems to her to be an impossible thing to do. Instinctively removing her driving gloves from her hands, stuffing them in her jacket pockets, and then also she removes her shoes. Placing her hand against the wall, she feels a strange adhesive of her hand to the wall, with now being able to climb she begins her ascend, as fast as she can, and begins to disappear into a large shadow the Police come to the very spot where she had been standing just seconds ago, one of them catches a glimpse of a leg disappearing into this shadow on the wall about ten feet up, sends a beam of light with his Flashlight up the wall, seeing nothing else, then hastily turns round to grab hold of his partner's shoulder, who's looking at the wall on the other side of the alley, and questions,

"Did you see that?"

"See what?"

As the officer points up at the wall, he states,

"I think, I just saw someone or something disappear into that shadow up there!"

"Up there! Are you nuts? What are we chasing Spider-Man?"

The officer looks at his partner and defendingly proclaims,

"Maybe not Spider-Man, but I tell ya, Frank, something went up this wall!"

"I think we should get going now, before the Hulk shows up, or the Batman."

As they start to leave one officer shines his Flashlight on the ground and claims,

"Wait, look at this!"

"Oh, what is it now?"

"Shoes!"

"Yeah, so, some bum lost his shoes."

"Frank, there Woman's shoes and they look fairly new!"

"So, come on, what do you want to do now, go scour the countryside looking to see who they belong to?"

"Oh, you mean like in Cinderella?"

"Come on, I'm going now. Are you coming? This is going to make one heck of a report."

"Well, I still say I saw something go up the wall!"

"Please, Derrick, don't put that in your report!"

"Frank, what about these two?"

"What? Two passed out drunken bums, come on, we'll leave them for the Hartford DPW to deal with in the morning."

Rachael gets to the rooftop and looks down saying softly,

"Looks like they've given up."

She looks around to see that there's a fire escape on the other side of the roof, making her way down, retracting her Vampire

Veneer, gets to the Street, takes a moment to compose herself, and getting her bearings, shifting her clothing, and brushing herself off, then heads in the direction of where she believes, she had parked her Car.

On the ride home, she reflects,

Wow, that was close, a little too close for comfort for me, maybe I'm getting a little too cocky, but at least I now know that the Hartford Police are looking into dead bodies being found drained of just about all their Blood, time to stop using Hartford or any big city for my feedings, for that matter. My Dad said something in his Memoir about staying local, feeding on people passing through Mystic, I'll review his Memoir once again when I get home, yeah home that sounds nice, right about now.

With that thought, she presses down on the gas pedal, accelerating to get herself home quicker once again.

Chapter Twenty-Five

AFTER TAKING HER jacket off Rachael sits in a Kitchen chair and removes the running shoes that she had put on, from where they were kept under her front Car seat, to make the drive home. She then gets up to get herself a glass of Wine, and sits back down and thinks aloud,

"I suppose it's a good thing I do keep these in the Car, but I should have worn them in the first place, instead of losing my favorite pair of Prada Pumps! But, I mean, who knew I'd have an encounter with the Hartford Police, guess I should have been more prepared for something like that happening, although it was strangely exciting to be able to outwit them!"

Marlena's voice chimes in,

"So you had a run in with the Police tonight?"

"Yeah, but I got away from them by using one of the powers, being a Vampire affords me!"

"And which one is that"?

Marlena asks.

"The one where I can scale a sheer wall like a spider… so cool!"

"That's great my Dear, but you may not be so lucky the next time."

"Well, Marlena there's not going to be a next time, at least not in Hartford or in any big City, I've decided to stay close to home from now on like my Dad did, and I surmise you had done also."

"Yeah, I would get, I mean meet all my victims at the Ebb Tide Restaurant Lounge, with the unsuspecting help of Nick, the bartender and the wait staff, of my true intentions."

"Didn't my Dad do something like that?"

"Well, yeah, but not at the Ebb Tide, he used the Pub that he frequented on Main Street, that later burnt down."

"Oh, yeah, that's right. What was it called?"

"I believe it was called the Lookout Sports Pub."

"Isn't that the place he and my Mom first met?"

"Yes, Rachael, they did, and not to long after that you were conceived!"

"How romantic, is that?"

"I would guess, you could look at it that way!"

"You guess! I can look at it any way I like!"

"Yes yes, my Dear any way you like no need to get all huffy about it with me!"

"I'm not getting huffy; I'm just still a little wired from the night's activities is all, I'm going to bed. Later Godmother!"

"Yes, my child, later."

Rachael rises from her chair, and quits the Kitchen, makes her way to the Grand Staircase to go up to bed, saying under her breath through clenched teeth,

"I hate it, when she calls me that."

***

Routinely on sunny days, like this one, Rachael spends these days in the house with all the windows shuttered, in order to keep the sun, now her enemy, out. She goes about her place cleaning, tidying up and doing laundry, although she'd like to, and intended to finish her novel, she's had Writer's Block for these last three months. Even her numerous **Blood Passion** feedings, with the help of Nick and his wait staff at the Ebb Tide Restaurant Lounge; by them introducing her to people, both men and women alike, that are passing through Mystic, on untraceable business Am-Track train trips using Mystic as an unscheduled stop over, so no one will know where it was that they went missing, has not given her any motivation to do any more writing of her novel.

Rachael takes a seat at her Kitchen table to rest awhile, with a glass of her favorite Wine, quickly now becoming the only liquid she can take in without feeling nauseous.

Suddenly, hears rapid ringing of the front door bell and loud banging on it. She peeks out of the Kitchen archway clearly through the Living Room to see that the oval cut glass window on the inside front door, reveals that it's her Mother, appearing rather irate. And yelling,

"Rachael, it's your Mother, come here right now, open this door and let me in or I'll open it myself!"

Rachael slowly walks to the door, answering her request loud enough for her to hear her,

"Chill out Mom, I'm coming!"

Opening the door, Mina bursts in with a few newspapers under her arm, throws them down on the floor, in front of Rachael, the one on the top of the pile, has the questioning headline of; 'VAMPIRES IN OUR MIDST?'. Mina then announces harshly,

"I see that my little Girl is making quite a reputation for herself in and around Connecticut and Rhode Island!"

"Mother, what on Earth, are you talking about?"

Mina points down at the pile of Newspapers on the floor and says,

"Rachael, don't play sly with me, just look, it's all over the papers, you know exactly what I'm talking about!"

Calmly Rachael answers,

"Well, if anyone would know, Dear Mother, what you are talking about it would be the Woman that created me, I'd have'ta say!"

"Are you saying that this is my fault?"

Rachael shrugs answering,

"Well, Mom, if the shoe fits."

"Shoe, what shoe?"

"Mom, for Crimney sake, it's just an expression!"

"Okay, oh yeah, Dear, but it's all over the papers, for the last three months about dead bodies being found in Hartford, and Providence with very little, to no Blood left in them, now you don't have to say that it's you doing this, but, if anyone knows that it's your handy work it would have to be me, after all that is what your Father did, I mean had to do to survive. And let's not forget about the one that washed up on a beach in Newport, Rhode Island a few months ago."

"Mom, please, you know that it was probably me, but no one else does."

"Rachael, probably **you**?"

"Well there's the…

"Rach, please!"

"Okay, yes, alright, yeah… it was me, but I needed the Blood to be able to live with my condition!"

"Your condition your condition, It's always been your condition."

"Mother, what do you want me to say? You of all people know that without the Blood I'll die! Is that what you want for me, to die? Or do you want me to be hung on a wall like how my Father died? Ah, or on a tree like I had to do to Marlena to keep her from killing, you and I."

"**What**! Now you're insinuating that **I**, killed your Father?"

"Well, If the Sh…!"

"Oh, not that shoe thing again!"

"No, Mom, I'm not saying that, but, it just sounds that way, is all."

"My Dear, Daughter, if this keeps up you may be caught, is all!"

"Mom, let me worry about that."

"You don't think that I worry about my one and only Daughter?"

"Of course I know you do! What I meant was, let me deal with it in my own way; I've been dealing with it since I was seven without your help."

"But Rachael you were only killing animals, back then!"

"Yes, Mom, but now I need Human Blood to sustain me, and I was using, the derelicts and the deviants of Hartford, and Providence for that."

"**Was using**! What are you using **now**?"

"Mom, it's getting late, don't you have to go pick up Mathew or something!"

Mina checks her Smartwatch and replies,

"Oh, my, yes, it's almost four, I was supposed to go food shopping for dinner, I must go, my Dear, and please say you'll be careful."

"As much as I can be."

So with a mutual hug and kiss Mina takes her leave of the Cliff House.

Rachael sits back down at the Kitchen table to finish her Wine and looks up at the ceiling proclaiming out loud,

"Marlena, I suppose you heard all that, and have something to say about it!."

She waits a few moments sipping her Wine, but there's no reply to her inquiry.

Leisurely turning in her chair to look out back through the somewhat sheer curtains on the back door, catching a glimpse of her bizarre Vampiric Raccoon Nemesis scurrying off into the wooded area of the Backyard dragging something in its mouth.

Declaring aloud,

"Ah, don't think for one minute, that I have forgotten about **you**! You little wretched Monster thingy! You just might be, my way out of all this. I only need to come up with a way to use you to my advantage."

And then thinks,

Okay Rach, time to use that superior intellect of yours.

Just at that moment, the Dryer buzzer sounds off in the Alcove, off the Kitchen.

So she declares,

"That plan will have to wait a little while, time now to get back to some of the somewhat normal things in my life."

Chapter Twenty-Six

RACHAEL SITS IN her Car, in the Ebb Tide Restaurant parking lot, thinking about what she will tell Lucy, that has been waiting in the lounge for her, after being put off for a few days for an explanation of what Rachael was doing out in the Backyard, on the evening that she showed up unannounced, just to see what her Bestie had been up to for the last six months, with no contact between them. Therefore, she starts to think,

I couldn't think of any answer to her on the spot, so I put her off with some lame excuse, not to explain my actions, with the promise to enlighten her, if she would meet me here tonight. She's always been like my shadow ever since we were little Girls at school. I do hate lying to her, or anyone, for that matter, just like my Dad says in his Memoirs. I'd guess that's just one more trait I've inherited from him, one of the more regular ones, I'd say, while all the others aren't so normal. Okay, now what can I tell her? I certainly can't reveal the truth to her, although I kinda wish I could, that I was disposing of one more of my many victims' dead bodies after acquiring all of its Blood for my survival. Well, yeah, really when I think about it, how could anyone live forever this way? Marlena just may be right about the moving around thing, endeavoring to stay one step ahead of the law.

****

On the night in question, Rachael was doing exactly what she recalls, but, just as she was to throw the body out over the Cliff, she was startled by hearing Lucy calling out to her from the back steps. Therefore, didn't lift it up over her head to pitch it out into the water to clear the rocks and be taken out to sea, but just let it drop over the edge, hurrying to get into the Backyard the long way round, by quickly but carefully walking along the Cliff's Edge length of the fence to the end where it stops at the property line to enter into her yard, through a low gate into her land, at the beginning of the thickly wooded area, never thinking to look back to observe, that the body was hung up on a protruding rock, which would make it visible from the water in the daylight.

And sure enough the next day a small boat with two men fishing came by close enough to take notice of a number of Seagulls gathered at something that appeared to them, as of what they could tell with all the birds alighting on it and hovering around it, it looked to them like a body hung up from a small rock ledge on the Cliff. When they finished their little fishing jaunt, and had made it back to shore, they reported what they had seen to the authorities, and went their way without a second thought about it.

The Police only half believing these men, assuming that maybe they may have had one to many beers, and had imagined it, did not respond right away, kind of taking it, rather lightly.

Rachael leisurely walks into the lounge, but before going over to where Lucy has been waiting at a table for her arrival, stops at the bar to get herself a glass of Wine from Nick.

She then goes to Lucy's table and sits, states and asks,

"Didn't see your Scooter in the parking lot, wasn't sure if you were here or not. How'd you get here? Take a Cab?"

"No, well, I'm drinking, so I had Jason drop me off!"

"That's Kool Beans!"

"Cool Beans?"

"Yeah, that's Kool with a K, it's what Shane would say when he really liked something, totally; I guess it kinda stuck in my head!"

"Did he say it a lot?"

"Well, he liked lots of stuff about me, like…"

"Rach, please, really no need to elaborate!"

"Lucy, I wasn't going to 'really' elaborate!"

"Good, now, Rach, what were you doing the other night in the Backyard? This, you can really elaborate on!"

"Okay, I take it you remember, the incident the night of the party, right, where you ventured into the wooded area of the yard, to go make out with Jason, and while waiting for him saw something that frightened you enough to call out to me so I came in to rescue you!"

"Yeah yeah, I remember! What's that have to do with you being out there the other night?"

"I believe I saw that Monster thingy you saw the night of the party, so, I was out there pursuing it!"

"What! Are you **crazy**?"

"Lucy, please, keep your voice down!"

Rachael declares, looking around the room.

"Lucy I know how to handle myself, so you need not worry about me."

"So, that's it, that's all?"

"Yeah, that's it. That's all it was. So, seeing that you're not driving yourself let me get you another drink."

Rachael offers, gesturing to the waitress for another round.

Their conversation continues with some light chit chat about the things going on in their lives.

After awhile, Lucy looks to check her Smartwatch to see that Jason should be by soon to pick her up. Doing this, it sounds off with a text from him saying that he's out in the lot waiting for her, so, Lucy rises and a hug is had, and she leaves the lounge. Soon after Rachael follows.

The subsequent day, at the Mystic Police Station, Captain Anderson, goes through the past few days front Desk reports, noticing the report about the two men observing what they believed was a body hanging from the Cliff, in the vicinity of the back of Thirty Cedar Lane. He calls in the officer of the day to confront him with this. Putting it out to him, he asks,

"Sergeant Walker, please sit, did you see this report?"

Walker takes it from him, and sits, takes a moment to read it over and says,

"Captain, surely this has to be a prank of some kind, I mean, Sir, a body hanging from the Cliff; I'd say, they must have been seeing things. Maybe, one two many Beers or too much Sun!"

"Regardless Walker, I want it checked out, promptly!"

"Will do, Sir, right away!" He answers as he gets up to leave.

Walker stops at the front Desk to put in a call to the Water Patrol Division to request that a Patrol Cruiser Boat meets him at the Main Street dock as soon as possible, they reply telling him it will be about an hour. In the meantime from his own Cruiser he radios the Police Cruiser for that area of Mystic that he just may be in need of their assistance, at the back of Thirty Cedar Lane. They reply in the positive. Walker then starts his Vehicle and heads for the Main Street Dock.

Chapter Twenty-Seven

POLICE SERGEANT WALKER steps on to the Mystic Police Launch and is greeted by its operator,

"Hey, Sergeant Walker, don't see too much of you around the Waterfront!"

"Yeah, Willy, I really don't like water!"

"And yet, you live and work in a Waterfront Town."

"That's true; can we get going, now?"

"Which direction, up current or down, Sir?"

"I'd say up, in the direction of the Cedar Road Peninsula."

"Well, you just have yourself a seat and we'll get under way."

As Walker finds himself a seat, Willy releases the boat, and it lurches forward, and then makes a quick U-turn to head up current.

"Hey, Walker what's this little trip all about?"

He tells him about the report. With that Willy lets out a laugh and says,

"Sounds to me like too many beers along with too much Sun."

"That's what I told the Captain, but he wants it checked out anyway."

"Well, we've a nice day for it!"

"So you say!"

"You can put on a life preserver if you're feeling unsafe; it is rule number one when on the water."

"Yeah, I know, and if I don't, what do I do arrest myself for breaking the rules?"

Again Willy lets out a laugh, throttles up and the launch goes into full speed. As the water Vehicle levels out and they slowly cruise along the shoreline to check the Cliffs, walker makes a call on the Boat's Radio to the Police Car in the area.

Officer Champa responds,

"This is Car Six, go!"

"Vince, is that you?"

"Yeah, with Officer Doyle, at your service!"

"I need you two to go to the vicinity of Cedar Lane, around number thirty or so."

"Will do! And...?"

"Wait there for further instruction."

"Okay, over and out."

Just as they approach the said area, Willy, with his Binoculars spots something that looks peculiar to him, he gets Sergeant Walker's attention,

"Hey Sarge, I just saw something reflective," he raises his arm to point, "On a ledge up there."

Walker takes the Binoculars to have a look for himself saying,

"I don't see anything. Maybe if we back up a little."

Willy replies,

"Sarge, hold on while I put her in reverse!"

As they slowly back up with Walker still watching the Cliff he proclaims,

"**There**! I see it **now**; pull us up to the shoreline, as close as you can, to the Cliff."

As the boat gets as close to the Cliff as it can without running aground, Walker still looking up through the Binoculars proclaims,

"We're too close; I can't see what's on the ledge from this angle."

"You want me to back up?"

Before Walker can answer a call from the Patrol Car comes over the radio,

"Hey Sarge, we're parked near Thirty Cedar Lane."

"Good, just sit tight for a while."

"Will do, Sir."

"Willy can you try angling the boat a little? So I can see what's on top of the ledge."

"I'm afraid that won't work Sarge, you'll need to look down from the top, to be able to see what it is!"

"Yeah, I guess you're right," he remarks as he picks up the Radio Mike and calls to the Car sitting on Cedar Lane,

"Champa, Doyle, you men there?"

"Yes we're here, Sir!"

"Good, now listen; you both need to make your way to the back of Thirty Cedar Lane and look down over the Cliff Edge and tell me what you see, because I can't see what's on the ledge from down here in the boat. You got that?"

"Yeah, but ain't that trespassing, Sir? I mean we don't have a warrant."

"Champa, we're the Police! All we need at this point, is just cause. Now go."

"Yes Sir!

As they begin to exit the Car, Walker abruptly instructs,

"Wait you two! Use the path of the adjoining property, and make your way to the Cliff's Edge in that manner."

"Okay, we're going now."

The two Officers slowly walk single file in the yard along the fence of the adjoining property, as they begin to enter the thickly wooded area, Officer Doyle leading the way, sees something he really can't explain and hastily draws his weapon, asking,

"Vince, did you see that?"

"See what?"

"I think I just saw someone, or **something** quickly dart behind that large tree!"

"**Something**?"

"Yeah **something**, because someone, would not have **red eyes**!"

"Did you say, **red eyes**?"

"Yeah, I said **red eyes**!"

"Oh, that's what I thought you said."

With his gun still out he announces,

"Look, there it is again!" And he fires a shot at it, striking the tree. He looks back at Vince and asks,

"Now don't tell me you didn't see that?"

"Well, I saw, and heard you shoot a tree, and I'm betting the whole neighborhood heard it!"

"Hey, I tell ya, I saw something!"

"We still need to get to the Cliff Edge and take a look over, for the Sarge."

As Officer Champa looks back from where they came, Officer Doyle fervently cries out,

"Look! There it goes under the fence into number thirty! Did you see it?"

"Sorry, I was looking back at the Car. What did it look like?"

"It was moving rather fast, all I could make out is, that it was somewhat large and black."

"Black? You mean like a person of color?"

"No, it definitely wasn't a person, I tell ya that, it was something else!"

"Maybe it was a Sasquatch, hah?"

"Now don't be silly Vince, it wasn't **that** big!"

"Ed, me! Be silly?" Vince then nudges his partner in the back and says, "Ed, put your gun away now, and let's get to the Cliff's Edge."

They slowly and alertly continue along the low fence, establishing their way to the end of it, where it will end at where the sergeant requested them to go.

Completely unaware of Rachael continuing to watch and listen to them, with piqued curiosity from her Kitchen window.

Chapter Twenty-Eight

"HEY, SARGE, WHERE are your men?"

Willy remarks questioningly.

"There'll be up there soon; I would guess that it's a little tricky walking along that edge, so they need to go slowly."

"Ah, I think I see them now, Sarge!"

Willy declares.

"Yeah, that's them," Sergeant Walker announces, and continues, "Doyle is that you?"

"Yes, and Officer Champa is right behind me, Sir."

"You men be careful up there on that edge, wouldn't want you falling!"

"Neither would I, Sarge,"

Officer Vincent Champa adds, as he comes into view of the two men down in the boat on the water.

"Hey, Sarge, just what are we looking for, from up here?"

Vince asks.

"Yeah, Sarge, what are we looking for? You never told us."

Officer Doyle reiterates.

"Although, actually we never did ask."

Vince chimes in.

"Just move a little further along the edge, and look down at the protruding ledge about fifteen, or so feet below you, and tell me if you see anything on it."

"Ain't much to see, looks like the remains of a body!"

Doyle remarks.

With noticed enthusiasm, Sergeant Walker inquires,

"Doyle, did you say a body? Is it a Human body?"

"Wait!" Officer Champa adds, "It's too small to be Human, Sarge, looks more like an animal of some kind, although it's pretty much, chewed up by the gulls, and anything else that could have got at it, I'd have'ta say. Sarge, how long ago was this reported being seen out here?"

"I really don't know exactly, the report was brought to my attention just this morning, it was dated by Desk Sergeant Howard about three days ago."

Willy lowers his boating magazine he's reading and adds,

"That's about enough time for the scavengers, and the elements to do a number on whatever it is or was!"

"Yeah, well, I'd guess we're done here men, you two up there take some pictures and print them out back at the station, add them in the report file, see you back there later, thanks for your assistants."

"Don't mention it Sarge, anytime you need us, we'll be there, after all it's our job!"

Officer Doyle replies.

"Okay, men, we're definitely done here, you and Champa go back on patrol and I'll see you both back at the station at the end of the shift," he then turns to Willy and orders, "okay Willy, get us back to the Main Street Dock, pronto."

With that said, Willy starts up the engine and heads back.

Officers Champa and Doyle carefully make their way back along the Cliff Edge with Champa leading the way to the end of the fence. Officer Champa notices some people out on Cedar Lane milling around their Patrol Car, he comes off the path taking a shorter way to the street and briskly walks threw the unkempt grass, without paying too much attention to where he's placing his feet, trips on some unseen item.

Ed catches a glimpse of him going down, and moves over quickly to where his partner is lying on the ground asking,

"Vince what are you doing down there?"

"Ed, what do you think I'm doing down here? Picking Daisies? Something tripped me up!"

Doyle extends his hand to help Vince up and they both look back to see what he tripped on, looking down, they see something that they find a little hard to believe, what they see is an animals' remains laying dead on its stomach. Vince picks up a broken branch and turns the thing over and notices that the body is strangely flat, almost like there's nothing inside of it, he then asks his partner to go to their Patrol Car and get, from the trunk, a pair of gloves and a plastic bag or two.

"Vince, what you planning on doing?"

"Ed, just get me what I asked for, we're taking this back to the station with us."

All the while, Rachael continues to observe their movements, and with her acute hearing taking in all that's being said. The sun is high in the sky, without any clouds to shield her from it, so she must remain in the house.

Ed calms down the people of the neighborhood that are hanging about the Police Patrol Cruiser, informing them saying that there's nothing for them to be concerned with and they should go about their business without any fears. As he makes his way back with the things his partner asked for, he himself is tripped up and falls, Vince gets to him and they both to their dismay see another dead animal.

"Vince it's another one. What the hell is going on around here?"

"Don't know partner, but we better have a look around to see if there's any more."

Ed drops the things he brought from the Car and they begin to walk carefully back toward the Cliff's Edge and as they do the wind shifts in their direction and the horrible stench of death fills their nostrils, making Ed retch and vomit.

"Man, there's a strong odor of death around here!"

Ed wipes his mouth on his sleeve, and answers,

"Yeah, tell me about it! Maybe we should get a team out here to scour this place."

"Oh, yeah, and start a panic in the neighborhood, and when it finds its way into the local papers that the Police are searching the area of the Cedar Road Peninsula for dead animals, the tourist trade in and around Mystic will dry up, and we'll get the blame! No way, buddy, we'll have'ta keep this between us for now. We'll take back the first two that we found, and see what Captain Anderson will want to do about it."

"Yeah, Partner, let the Captain take the flack!"

They go back to get the things that Ed brought from the Car and gather up the first two dead ones, quickly loading them into the trunk and speeding off to the station.

Rachael seeing everything and hearing it all thinks out loud,

"That's not my doing; it's that darn Vampiric Raccoon's leavings, drawing attention to the neighborhood and my place."

As Officers Vince Champa and Ed Doyle ride back to the station, Officer Doyle looks over to his partner, Officer Champa and having a thought he asks,

"Thirty Cedar Lane, hey, Vince didn't someone in your family, own that place at one time?"

"Yeah, my Grandfather's older Brother Romeo built it back in the forties, so my Mom has told me."

"Vince, I understand he was a very rich Man."

"Yes, Ed, he was, he owned quite a bit of land around here almost the whole Cedar Road Peninsula. All this land he had acquired real cheap back in the forties, before his street was named Cedar Lane, once that was done, he then sold it off a little at a time for a tidy profit for himself, but I never saw any of that money! So my Mom, once again has told me the whole story about it, and how he had asked my Granddad, Giuseppe to invest with him, but my Granddad; at that time didn't think it was a sound investment."

"Too bad for you, hah?"

"Well, Romeo died some time ago, and the Cliff house, as its come to be called, and all he had went to his only child, my first cousin, Carmella Valli."

"Vince, I seem to remember that a young Man named Michael Valli lived there for awhile, and then suddenly disappeared without a trace!"

"Yeah, that's in the files, to this day, as an unsolved case!"

"You ever talk to this Carmella cousin of yours?"

"No, not really, she was married young, and moved away to Rhode Island to live with her husband Michael Valli, Sr."

"I do remember seeing the missing persons report about her son sometime ago, which would be your second cousin Michael, Jr., right?"

"Yeah, Ed that would be right, but she never came to me about it!"

"That's all too sad, Vince."

"Yeah Ed, her only child, Michael was a young Man, when he went missing, but we weren't a very close knit family to begin with."

Their conversation is interrupted, as they pull into the parking area at the back of the Police Station, where they then proceed to get the evidence out of the trunk and into the evidence room. Then make their way upstairs to fill out their Reports. As they start writing, Sergeant Walker walks in and greets them saying,

"Quite the little mystery out there today, men?"

Officer Champa looks up and adds,

"Yeah, Sarge, but there's more."

"More? Vince, like how much more?"

Officer Champa informs him of what they came upon after they left the Cliff's Edge and that they have brought in two of the items.

Walker raises an eyebrow saying,

"Interesting men! I'll have'ta follow up on this with the Captain."

Chapter Twenty-Nine

RACHAEL WATCHED FROM the inner front door as the Police Car disappeared over the low rise in the road of Cedar Lane, back to the Kitchen, tops off her glass of Wine and takes a seat at the table, and begins to consider,

I will have to hazard a guess that the Mystic Police Department will start poking around here soon, looking to see why all the dead animals are out there, which means my place will be under scrutiny by the Polices' watchful eyes.

She takes in a large swallow of her Wine and continues in her line of thought,

I'll need to craft a plan, to most likely leave Mystic and the whole state of Connecticut, as much as I Love being here, and will miss my family, my disappearance has to be in away that no one will suspect me of any wrong doing and try to come looking for me.

She takes another large swallow of her Wine, and just sits in silence, with her elbow on the table with her chin resting in the palm of her hand, contemplating.

***

Sergeant Walker enters the Police Lab; the attending Forensic Officer for the New London County stops his examination of one of the animals to greet him,

"Sergeant Al Walker, if my memory serves me, long time, we don't see much of you down here in the Forensic Departments!"

"Yeah, Hank, I don't get too many cases, that require your expertise. But this one, is a strange one!"

"Not seeing me here too much is probably a good thing for you and your little quaint Waterfront Town of Mystic."

"I guess you could put it that way. Do you have anything to tell me about these dead animals, yet?"

"What I've found so far, Sergeant is really quite strange, both these carcasses are vacant of any Blood."

Sergeant Walker puts down the scalpel he's looking at, and immediately turns round proclaiming,

"Did you just say that these animals haven't any Blood left in their bodies? I mean how is that possible, Hank?"

"Not sure exactly, but even if they had been out there for some time, there'd still be a trace; these two have no Blood in their bodies that I can detect. It's like some thing sucked it out of them. Oh, and there is a faint sign of puncture wounds on their neck on both of them. Here take a look for yourself, if you doubt me."

"No that's alright, Hank, I'll pass! But come on, are you telling me that there's something out there sucking the Blood of animals? Like, like… a Vampire?"

"Something, or someone, Sarge, but that's not my call, you people would need to find that out, before I'll make any mention of it in my report."

"Good, you just hold off on reporting, or saying any thing like that, until we know for sure, we wouldn't want to scare off the tourists, now would we, Hank?"

"No, Sarge we certainly wouldn't want that!"

"I'll see about putting together a crew, to make a search of the area, as soon as possible, to see just what we can find out!"

As Walker quits the Lab, Hank calls out to him,

"You had best make it a Haz-Mat crew, Sarge!"

He hears Walker reply,

"Yeah, okay!"

Then he faintly hears him continue saying as he's walking further down the hall.

"This is all too weird for me, maybe the Captain can make some sense of it?"

With Walker out of earshot, Hank, says under his breath,

"Yeah, Walker, you pass the buck."

***

I will need to get as far away from my beloved Mystic, but just before I decide to leave, I'll need to make it look like I have died, fake my own death somehow, wait, maybe I could use that damn Mutant Raccoon, but really kill it, wouldn't want to leave it alive here to run a muck, have'ta stage it to look like we killed each other. Yeah, it would be 'killing two birds with one stone'.

Rachael pours herself some more Wine continuing to conjure her plan in her mind.

I'll need to make some preparations for my disappearance first; I'm going to need to take all my money with me, there are a few duffel bags in the Basement, I can certainly use them for that, also I can't take any of my clothes or personal effects, once I'm safely away, I'll stop and get some more clothes and things. Oh wait! The Car! I'll need to take it, and if it's gone that will also look like I just took off, so just before I go, I will have to report it stolen, having an out of town Mechanic take it in his shop for a tune-up or oil change or something like that, so when the Police do come to make a stolen Car Report, it won't be here, then on the day before I go, I'll have to use one of those unregistered Car Services, they never keep any records of to whom they carry to anywhere, to go retrieve it. Then when I've made my nocturnal get away, I'll leave it somewhere near New London, and then rent another, go back to where I left it, transfer the money bags and then disappear, clean away! Okay, well, this all sounds great in theory, but will it really work? I'll also need a fake I.D., and I know exactly who to call for that.

Well, most of this is going to take money, and I certainly have more that enough for that.

She breaks off from her mental planning saying,

"I'd better get started on acquiring my new credentials. Now where'd I put my personal, private phone book? Oh, yeah, in my Desk, I'm sure, the Police won't waste too much time starting their investigation, although it will give me some extra prep time if they start with the yard next door. And speaking of my Desk, no one really knows what I usually keep in there, so I certainly can take with me, most of what's in it. Okay, Rach, you're talking a little too much to yourself. What is it they say, about people who do that?"

Chapter Thirty

"**CRAZY**! THAT'S WHAT they say, that you're **Crazy**! When you talk to yourself too much, it's been said that you're **Crazy**, or you have money in the bank, well all my money is here with me, so for me, it just might be that I am the former! So that would mean that I'm nuts, bonkers, out of my mind, gone round the bend!"

"You're not crazy, nuts, or any of those things, Child, you're just a little lonely, and somewhat distraught!"

Marlena's haunting voice answers her query.

"Marlena! Where've you been?"

"Here and there!"

"Doing what?"

"Oh, this and that!"

Ever the evasive one!

Rachael thinks and then says,

"I really shouldn't bother to ask you for details about your absences, I should know by now not to. Lonely, yes, I am a bit, but I suppose I'll need to get use to it being my way of living, unless I can find or create someone like myself, I would think! But, not so much distraught, Godmother, I do have the makings of a plan."

"I didn't get to hear your plan, might be I could help you with it. You could, or anyone that really knew me in life would say that, I **was** quite the schemer, if I do say so myself."

"I will tell you all about it, and if you have anything to add, or find any holes in it, I'd be open to your input. Just let me go to the Kitchen, and get some more Wine, and when I get back, I'll fill you in on all that has occurred, in your absence."

"If this is going to take awhile, you'd better bring the bottle!"

As Rachael heads out of the Library answering,

"Yeah, good idea! Be right back!"

Rachael finishes telling Marlena the whole of what has transpired and all about her plan to disappear, sits back in the Desk chair, clasps her hands behind her head and asks,

"So, what do you think?"

"Please, child, let me study on it for a bit, then I'll give you my views of your plight."

"Okay, I've something to attend to while you consider it all."

"Good, my Dear, when you are done with that, come back here to the Library, and we'll continue."

Rachael goes off to the Alcove Laundry Room off the Kitchen in the attempt to make a private call,

"Hello, hi, it's me, I need a favor!"

A Man's voice on the other end of the phone responds,

"Yeah, hun I know who this is, what is it that you want of me?"

"It's not so much what I want, of you, more of what I need, you to do for me."

"Not quite following you, please be more specific?"

"Yeah, okay, I need without any questions asked a new I.D., secrecy is required, and price is no object. So what do you say?"

"Never, has there been a problem doing anything for you, Sweetie! I'll need a picture of you, of course, bring it to me just as soon as you can. Okay?"

"I'll need for you to take the picture, although it may not look exactly like me, as you know me, some changes will be needed, like my hair and eye color."

"Okay, you take care of the hair color, I'll supply the eye color change, when you come by to take the picture, get back to me when you're ready."

Good, thanks in advance, in touch soon, bye!"

She hangs up, gets the bottle of Wine, and her glass from the table then heads back to the Library. Places the bottle and glass on her Desk sits down and pours herself a glass, picks it up sits back, and says,

"Well Godmother, have any input on my plan?"

She waits a moment and finally gets a response to her query,

"My Dear, it all sounds pretty good, except for a few things, and by the way you look a little drawn and pale."

Rachael restlessly answers,

"I know, I'm slightly overdue for a feeding, I do believe I'll have'ta chance a quick trip to Hartford tonight."

"Well be careful, when you return we'll continue with our discussion."

"Yeah, I'm going up to dress for my outing."

Marlena advises her,

"No heels!"

As Rachael ascends the Grant Staircase answering,

"Yeah, I know, thanks, talk later.

***

Later for them both, arrives in about two and a half hours subsequently, Rachael walks in the back door with a pair of heel slung over her shoulder, continuing on into the Library, lollops into the large reading chair with the shoes in her hand draped over the arm of the chair.

Marlena begins with a question,

"What's this you stopped to buy a pair of heels?"

"Lena, you really think I had time to go shopping?"

"Well, wait; is that the pair of…?"

Rachael cuts her off with,

"As unbelievable as it may seem, the homeless Woman that had the unfortunate fate of being my most recent victim, was wearing them! So, I took her Blood, and got my, favorite Prada designer pumps back!"

Marlena lets out a haunting laugh, and says,

"Well, that's great, and you do look better!"

"And feel better, too, as you yourself should remember."

"Please don't remind me. You think I wanted to live like that? I mean, because of it, I lost my children, and took my beloved husband's…"

Marlena stops mid-sentence.

Rachael questions,

"Marlena, took your husband's what?"

"Oh, never mind! Forget that I said anything."

"Wait, you **did**!"

"**Did** what?"

"My Mother and I always suspected that you **did**."

"Suspected? Suspected that I **did** what?"

"That you killed your husband, James, so he didn't run off with his secretary Susan, after all, like you told everyone. Did he, Lena?"

With sadness in her voice she responds,

"No, he didn't, and I don't want to talk about it!"

With that said, Marlena quickly changes the subject,

"Rachael, child, I've been giving your plan some more thought while you were out on your little jaunt, and found a few things I'd like to bring to your attention."

"Okay, Godmother just let me get a fresh bottle of Wine, and then you'll have my full attention!"

As Rachael exits the Library, Marlena proclaims,

"Rachael, it's so nice that you still look upon me as your, Godmother."

Rachael says back, as she keeps walking out of the Library archway toward the Kitchen,

"Well, you are, were, I mean was, oh… whatever!"

Chapter Thirty-One

"Mia, try not to be so nervous, they will be able to detect it from you," Marcus says, in an effort to calm her, "Keep the hood of your robe up and stay behind me, if I must introduce you, it will be as Selena, my concubine."

"Okay, but I'm still a little frightened of the whole thing. But loving you as much as I do, I'll try to do as you say."

"Good, they want me to make a statement on the subject of becoming their new leader, of which, I never wanted, as I told you, I'm the next in line to inherit the title, I will make the attempt to bestow it on to my twin Brother Victus, hoping Quintus will agree to my proposal, and if not I will have'ta except, and then concede to Victus."

"I do hope it goes the way you want. Will there be many of them there?"

"Yes, my Love, the complete membership of the Cabal should be in attendance, but please, like I said, try not to be frightened, they mean us no harm."

"What will happen to you Marcus? If, and when they accept your refusal to be their leader?"

"At that moment you and I will be free to go where ever we wish," Marcus sees a sign of doubt in Mia's eyes, "No, my Love, they will not pursue us, I assure you it will be over, I… we will be free to live as we so desire!"

"Can you then make me like you?"

"If that is what you wish, yes!"

"Rachael! Rachael!"

She is interrupted, from her writing by hearing her name emulating from everywhere in her Bedroom.

"Yes, Lena, what is it?"

Rachael response slightly agitated.

"So sorry to disturb you, but I thought we were going to discuss your plan, I do have some thoughts about it!"

"Well, I came back to the Library, and you were gone, to where, I won't even try to fathom a guess."

"My Dear, I would still like to think, that I have some kinda life, or afterlife, or spiritual life."

"Yeah, leave it to you to still try to mingle, with the living."

"Mingling was my Specialty."

"Yeah Marlena, so my Mom has told me! All right then, what do you have for me?"

"I've found a few weak points to your plan."

"Oh, yeah, like what? Pray tell!"

"There are people in your life that know you have a Laptop, and things you will want to keep, so if you are going to take them with you, you'll need to say that they were in the Car when it was taken."

"Okay, good, any thing else?"

"Oh, yes, you will have to do some damage to my beautiful Classic Automobile!"

"Your Car! Your Sister, Mattie gave it to me. Or didn't you know that?"

"Well, okay then, **your** beautiful Classic Automobile!"

"Damage, like what?"

"Smash the driver's side window, and make it look like it's been hot wired. Can you do that?"

"Yeah, I've seen Bobby hot wire his Car lots of times!"

"And why would he hot wire…oh never mind!"

"Well, I think that's about it for now."

"For now?"

"Yes if I think of anything else, I'll let you know!"

With that being said, Rachael goes back to her Manuscript;

Mia puts her hands on Marcus's hips as she walks close behind him.

They enter the large gathering hall slowly and stop about ten feet in front of a large chair on a pedestal; this chair looks more like a throne, with it being trimmed with what looks to be gold inlay. There are also some large glittering jewels in some places.

Suddenly a loud gong is sounded, and anyone that is seated rises swiftly, and from the back of this throne a hooded person appears. This person is handed a long staff by an attendant, then bangs it three times on the floor and then sits down, and the room goes totally silent, you could hear a pin drop!

This person on the throne pushes back their hood to reveal a very old face, I mean really old, looks to be ageless, I couldn't even guess at how old, also I'm not sure if its a Man or a Woman, could this be Quintus that Marcus talks about? Or just someone sitting in judgment, like a Magistrate of some kind.

"Marcus step closer please."

He slightly turns his head back to me and whispers,

"Stay close with me, and make not a sound."

We move slowly forward in unison, like as one person, Marcus than gives a slight bow of respect from his waist and it's like the whole room is holding its breath for the next word to be spoken!

"Marcus I'm so pleased you chose to come here of your own volition."

"You mean, and not dragged her by Lucas!"

"Yes exactly that, it was not something I wanted to witness!"

"I do realize how important this all is, so I came to make my intentions clear!"

"I now give you leave to do just that!"

"Thank you, Quintus."

Mia thinks, so this is Quintus! Marcus makes his claim as plain as he can, that he requests to relinquish the throne to his twin Brother, for he has no wish to be leader of the Cabal at this time.

Quintus lowers his head to look down, and when after what seems like a long while, he rises to look at the gathering again, and he proceeds to proclaim his judgment loud and clear;

"Marcus my Dear Boy, I will grant your request on one condition."

"And that is, Sir?"

"That will be, if anything should happen, that your Brother can not continue to lead, you will immediately step in with out question! Will you give me your word on this stipulation?"

"By all means, **yes**!*"*

*"***Good!*** Then I now call this gathering to a close, lets all drink on it!"*

I whisper to Marcus questioningly,

"Drink?"

He quickly turns round to me, and articulates,

"Wine!"

I sigh in relief of what it, might have been if not Wine.

As we sip our Wine Marcus gets close to me and whispers to me,

"We, Mia, are now free to go where we wish, whenever we want."

"And my Love, how soon will that be?"

"Let's get a good night sleep, and we shall leave in the morning without anyone in pursuit of us."

"Sounds great to me, I really do Love you, Marcus!"

And I, you, Mia!"

Chapter Thirty-Two

RACHAEL IS AWAKENED at about eleven in the morning, by the loud slamming of a Vehicle door and raised voices; emerging from her bed, adorns herself with her robe, and quickly makes her way out into the hallway to the window at the front of the House. Parked on Cedar Lane to the right of the Cliff House, in front of the sparsely wooded vacant lot between her place, and next door, observing a large black panel Van with the markings in large white lettering, NEW LONDON HAZ-MAT Services, and two Mystic Police Cruisers. A person in a bright yellow suit that covers them completely, with raised hands says to Sergeant Walker,

"Sir, it will be necessary for you and your men to stay out here on the street, you, and they are not protected from any toxic harm, that we may encounter, and you Sir, and your men can help keep the residents calm."

Rachael has an agitated thought,

So the Mystic Police with the aid of a New London authority's service have started their investigation! That just means, I'll have to accelerate my plan to disappear a little sooner than I'd like. I'll need to find an out of town service station to pick up my Car on a flatbed truck and take it in for a tune-up and such. But first, my new identity, time to call Bobby's older Brother Billy again, to tell him I'm ready for him to render me his services. After all that, I'll need to bait the little Monster living in my Backyard to stage a fight and make it look like we both went over the Cliff together and fell to our death in the struggle!

Rachael observes the Haz-Mat team, to see them gather up some of the dead animals and samples of earth, they finish up at about two. She hears Sergeant Walker being told that they will be back in a few days if they find anything that they have collected that would be hazardous to the people or the environment, and that the area should be taped off until it is given the all clear. Walker agrees, so gives the order to his men to do just that.

While watching all this, she has an inspiring thought,

Wait a tic; I won't have to die my hair! I can use one of Marlena's wigs that I held on to. I think the blond one will do nicely; I'll go get it and see how it fits me.

After trying on the wig, and seeing that it will do nicely. She makes the call to Billy, and sets up an appointment with him for later that evening. In the meantime, she'll go on the web to find an out of town service garage for the Car to be gone when reports it stolen. So after she disappears, it will explain why the Car is gone, and raising no suspicions that she had just drove off in it.

She has a taxing thought,

This will take precise planning, if I'm going to pull this off successfully and have people believe that I've died, so sorry that it will be painful to my Loved ones, but I can't have anyone looking for me, they ***must*** *truly believe that I'm dead, and gone!*

All this planning, and thinking weighs heavily on her mind, and emotions, leaving all the people in her life that she Loves, and cares about, will not be as easy as she thought it would. But the situation calls for these drastic measures. She will have to find the emotional strength to accomplish it because if caught and taken into custody, she would most definitely be incarcerated and executed. Her plan hinged on the aid of a Ghost, and not a very trustworthy one at that. She truly felt;

Thank goodness, Marlena can't read my thoughts.

She shakes off the melancholy feelings and proclaims,

"Okay, first things first, find an out of town Service Station to take the Car, and the further away the better!"

Checking the internet; she finds Ritchie's Repair and Detailing Shop, up north, in Hebron, far enough away to be on the safe side. She takes note of the contact number, in which she will call soon.

****

Rachael arrives at the appointed time at Billy's apartment building on Main Street, parks her Car in the lot that is on the water's edge at the back of the building. At the foyer of the building, rings his bell. Within a minute he buzzes her in and she makes her way to his second floor apartment. He greets her in the hallway and is somewhat surprised at what he sees, so he declares,

"Hey Rach, ya do look quite different with blond hair, please come in, and I'll fit you with some contact lenses that will change your eye color. You did say blue, right?"

"Yes, I did, I believe with blond hair, blue eyes will seem more natural. Don't you think?"

"Yeah, I would agree."

He hands her the contacts and after putting them in, raises her face to him and says,

"So, what do you think?"

"Wow! You don't look like the Rachael I know!"

"That's exactly the effect I will need!"

"This effect is for what purpose? May I ask?"

"No you may not, it's a little secret!"

"Okay, but it's all a little weird to me for you to be doing this!"

"Why would you think that it's strange for me to do something like this?"

"I don't know, but it feels odd!"

He takes the pictures of her, with her new look and creates the new identifications, she will need. It all takes but a few minutes with his equipment.

"Here's the money that we agreed on, thank you for helping me with this."

"I'm not so sure of what I'm helping you with, but thanks, you're very welcome. Is it for some kind of prank you're playing on someone?"

Rachael has a quick thought,

He's far too nosey for his own good, I don't think I should leave him with this knowledge; just might become, a loose end! And I really should cover my tracks, and could use a feeding right about now, so…

"Billy, would you put all this on a flash drive I have with me please and walk me down to my Car? I noticed when I came in that the lights in the parking lot were out and it feels a little menacing back there to me."

"Sure, no prob, on both requests!"

They approach her Car together, parked at the far end of the lot very close to the retaining wall at the water's edge, where you can hear the Mystic Bay water slapping up against it. He puts out his hand in the act to say goodbye, with her back to him to unlock the Car door, bringing out her Vampire Veneer, swiftly turning around giving him a hug and softly whispering in his ear,

"Thanks, again, for everything."

Then holds on to him dreadfully tight, and sinks her fangs into his neck rapidly sucking out about two pints of his Blood, which makes him collapse into her arms, where she finishes him off, shifting around to let his lifeless body lay slowly to the curb top of the low retaining wall, then reaches into his jeans pocket to take back the money given him, with very little effort slides this empty vessel off the low curb and into the water, which makes no sound at all. Feeling no remorse, and taking a quick look round to see no one is about, then opens the Car door and enters it, retracts her Vampire attributes, and heads for home with the thought of,

All right, phase one complete. Next!

Chapter Thirty-Three

RACHAEL PUTS HER Wine glass down on the Library Desk to dial the number for the Car Service Station; suddenly stops, lays her Cell-phone down on the Desk, having these thoughts,

I can't have them come here to get the Car, I'll need to take it to them, then get an anonymous Car Service to bring me back, but not here to the Cliff House, I'll have them drop me off on Main Street, I can then walk home from there, I'll do this part under the guise of my new identity. And when they are done with it, I'll pick it up with another Car from the same service, I'll pay all the costs in cash and bring it back here to stash in my garage, there being no windows on the building anywhere, no one can look in, and see it looking all shiny and new, then I'll stage my death, and be on my way, yeah that should work nicely. Eventually, but sadly discarding the Car somewhere on my way out of Connecticut, crashing it into a wooded area-kind of hidden-as if it had been stolen, and in an accident, not far from a local town, close enough to walk to, obtaining anyway, I have too, -rent, buy, or whatever, -another Car, to make my way back to it to get my stuff, then I can be on my way for good. I think maybe I've that part worked out. So many details I really do hope this is actually going to work! Yes, it will work, it has to work, it must work, its gotta work. Details, details, details!

Marlena's voice suddenly chimes in from nowhere; startling her making Rachael almost spill her Wine, as her voice brings her out of these ranting thoughts.

"So do you have the details of your escape plan figured out, yet?"

"I just hate when you do that!" Rachael angrily retorts, and continues with a question, "Why can't you manifest yourself before talking?"

"I just Love surprises! Don't you?"

"**No**, Marlena I don't, and I'd appreciate it if you'd not do that anymore, please."

"So, my Dear, what is left to do in your plan?"

"Okay, I've my new identity, so that part is finished, next is to have to decide where the Car gets stolen from, I really don't think it should be from here, I'm thinking maybe from the parking lot behind the stores, on Main Street would be best. What do you think, Marlena?"

"The parking lot sounds better, that way it's not totally connected to you, here at the Cliff House. What else is there in your plan?"

Well, the key item is to confront the Monster Raccoon in the Backyard at the Cliffs' Edge, where I can stage a fight in which it will look like we both fell to our deaths!"

"I believe, you expect to win this conflict, right?"

"Of course I do, without a doubt!"

"Are you as confident as you sound?"

"**Yes**! **Very**."

"By the way, what is this new identity of yours?

"Okay, so after I have the Car back from the Car Service People, because I do want it running and looking its best for its last ride, I'll hide it in my garage. Then, as my real self I'll walk to Main Street, do a little shopping, then go into the parking lot to an empty space, call the Police on my Cell-phone to report that my Car is gone, then get back here to the house to plan the next step."

"Rachael, my Dear, don't you think you've had enough Wine for now?"

"Had enough Wine? I'll be the judge of that, thank you very much!"

"Have you made the arrangement for when the Car will be taken, to this Car Repair and Maintenance Place?"

"Oh Dear, no, not yet, I seem to be getting a little ahead of myself. But I've changed that part a little, it won't be taken, I'll be bringing it there myself"

"But while you are ahead of yourself, let me ask you this."

Rachael answers, after a large swallow of her Wine.

"Ask me what?"

"What's this new identity of yours? And just how do you intend to bait this thing you call a Monster?"

Rachael once again ignores Marlena's identity question and continues,

"I've the idea, to use a trail of my own Blood, to the Cliff Edge on the other side of the fence, of course! And Marlena, my new identity is on a need to know basis only, and **you** don't need to know."

"Rachael, whom am I going to tell? So you truly believe that your Blood will be too enticing for it to pass up, if it's in need of it?"

"Oh, it's not a question of need; it's more of a question of want, Dear Godmother!"

"Want?"

"Yes, want!"

"How so?"

"In my observations on its feeding behavior, it's come to my attention that it doesn't get to have Human Blood on any regular basis, so mine would be quite a treat, I would surmise!"

"Yeah, I would have to say, that sounds about right."

Rachael takes a long drink of her Wine and answers her sarcastically.

"I'm just oh sooo… glad you agree. Okay then, I do, really need to ca ca call the Car repair place to make the arrangements now, so if you'll excuse me for awhile, please be gone."

With that said Marlena's ethereal image dissipates.

With a large swallow, empties her glass of Wine, then goes and gets herself another bringing the bottle back with her, sits back down at the Library Desk to make the call, a Female voice answers announcing,

"Hello Richie's Car Repair and Detailing Services!"

"My na na name… I mean I'm calling about having my Car serviced and detailed by you people."

"Yes, how soon do you want this to be done, and what make and model Vehicle is it?"

"Well, as soon as possible, it's my beautiful 1954 MG Midget Sports Car. That won't be a problem will it?"

"Please, hold on a minute."

The Woman lowers the phone and covers the mouthpiece of her phone with her hand, Rachael can, just about, make out what she's asking someone.

"Richie, can you work on…."

After a brief hold, this woman comes back on the phone,

"So sorry about that, I'm back, that by no means, is a problem, can you get it here by Tuesday? You will need to leave it with us."

"About how la long will it take?"

"That depends on what you want done, of course."

"Well, let me see, I want the works, she's a gorgeous Automobile, and I'd like her to be running perfectly, and by the way, price is no object. I'll bring the Car to you Tuesday afternoon, you can call me when it's ready to be picked up and I'll come get it, and I will be paying with ca cash!"

"That will be perfectly fine! We'll see you then, bye."

"Yes, thank you"

Rachael hangs up, takes in a large swallow of her Wine and thinks,

Phase two is nearly ready to be executed, I should be set for phase three real soon. Now let me see, what's next for phase two? I'll need to call the anonymous Car Service, that my Step-Dad, Joseph would use from time to time, so as to have them come get me at this Riches' place.

She then makes the call to the private Car Personal Transport Services, making the arrangement; for them to come get her at Riches' place after leaving her Car with them, and then bring her back to Mystic, dropping her off on Main Street, also telling them that she'll need them again, when her Car is finished, and ready to be picked up.

Rachael proclaims out loud,

"So, phase two is re ready for Tuesday."

Marlena's haunting voice emanates loudly in the room,

"The best laid plans of..."

"Oh, shut-up do! Marlena!"

As Rachael walks somewhat ineptly up the Grand Staircase with her glass and bottle of Wine in tow, having some repetitive thoughts,

My plan will work, I know it will work, it has to work, it's going to work!

When reaching the top turns in the direction of her room and with each carefully placed step, thinking,

Work! It! Will! Work! Work! It! Will! Work! It! Will! Work! Work!

When reaching her Bedroom door, fumbling with the Doorknob finally getting it open, staggering in, her thoughts end with her saying aloud,

"It has to work! It will... will... so work!"

After roughly putting the bottle down on her vanity table, knocking over most of her make-up bottles, then emptying her glass with one last big swallow; without looking, puts the Wine glass down, right on the edge of the table where it falls to the floor. While lolloping herself down on her bed saying,

"Ug, I don't feel so good. But my plan is going to work... perfectly!"

She keeps repeating the word perfectly, as it fades softer and softer until finally passing out.

Chapter Thirty-Four

RACHAEL FINDS HERSELF standing in what is a pitch black abyss, she can't see any walls or a ceiling or for that matter, her hand in front of her face, but under her feet seems solid enough, far off in what seems to her like the distance she sees a small fuzzy white shiny thing coming at her getting closer and closer gradually. She tries hard to focus to see what it could be; as it gradually comes closer it begins to get a bit larger and slightly clearer.

This unrecognizable thing speaks shrilly to her with a voice that appears to sound neither Male nor Female, rather like somewhere in between.

"**Rachael**!"

She is somewhat shaken, that try as she might she can't bring out her Vampire defences, but finds it within herself to answer, and ask,

"Yes, that's my name. How do you…? Oh, who or what, are you?"

"Who, or what I am, is not important, what I can do for you, is!"

"Oh, and what can you do for me?"

"I can help you get away safely."

"**You** can do that, how? That would be great, thank you, but I think I have it all taken care of."

"**She** is trying to make you fail and get yourself caught, please you must believe me, I know how devious **she** can be with someone **she** only pretends to like, and care about, but actually despises, please oh please, you must believe me."

"I'm sorry, but I find it a little hard to believe someone, or something, when I don't know who, or what it is!"

"I told you that who I am is not important, please you must believe me, and take heed of my warning."

"So then, you are, a who, and not a what."

"Yes yes! I was… now please you must listen…"

"Rachael, Rachael, **Rachael**!"

She is awoken by the sound of Marlena calling her name.

Opening her eyes, she sees Marlena hovering above her, she begins to lift her head, when a painful throbbing starts, so she lays it back down and it diminishes. She places her hand gently on her forehead softly proclaiming aloud,

"Oh, my aching head! This is what a hangover must be, strangely, the Wine has never affected me like this before, must be a change in my condition, maybe more of my Human side showing through. Don't know if that's a good thing or a bad thing."

"Do hate to upset you my Dear, but your Human side can be more a hindrance than a help. Take it from one who knows!"

"What's that suppose to mean?"

Marlena answers her evasively,

"Mean? Well, you know that, I've been there so I'm one who knows. Now, aren't I?

"Yes, I suppose so!"

Rachael slowly gets herself up, and sits on the side of her bed moaning, and holding her head, saying softly,

"Gee, my head feels three times its normal size."

"I do have a remedy for that,"

Marlena gently informs her, and instructs,

"If you can get yourself down to the Kitchen, I'll explain to you on how to make something that will make you feel much better."

"Yeah, I think I can do that, but very slowly."

"That will be fine; I'll see you down there."

Rachael slowly sips the concoction that Marlena instructed her to make. After a few moments, with Rachael having drunk about half of it, Marlena gently asks,

"So are we feeling a bit better now, my Dear?"

"A little, yes, thank you. Remind me never to drink that much Wine ever again."

"Yes, for at least while we're still in contact with each other."

The rest of the day finds Rachael recuperating from her over indulgence of Wine, and going over her plan. Knowing that tomorrow is Tuesday, the day she is supposed to deliver her Car to the shop, she will need to have her wits about her, so will use the day to rest and recover.

Gloomy Tuesday morning finds her, feeling her old self once again. She leaves the house and drives north to the shop to deliver her Car; only to stop briefly on the way, somewhere in a secluded place to apply her eye color changing contacts, and put on her blond wig, as not to look like her real self. The call for the Car Service to come get her and drop her off on Main Street, downtown Mystic is all arranged.

The next five days go by uneventfully; on the morning of the sixth day, in which is another cloudy Autumn day in New England, the shop contacts her to come retrieve her Car. After accomplishing that she begins to make ready for her get-away, by first filling the two duffel bags from the basement with all the cash that they will hold. She gathers any thing else She believes She can take with her and puts it all in the Car; that is now hidden in her garage, all fueled and ready to go. Tomorrow afternoon, yet another overcast day, as her real self, she'll walk down to Main Street, do some shopping then go to the parking lot stand in an empty space and call the Police to report that her Car is gone.

Then walk back home to bait the Vampire Raccoon, stage the confrontation, and in the night, under the cover of darkness make her nocturnal get away.

As the night slowly closes in, and after taking herself a leisurely walk through the house having her last look around, She goes out back to the porch, seating herself on one of the cement benches, with her Great-Grandfathers hunting knife making a cut in her arm, and as the Blood begins to flow, slowly walking, creating a trail of her Blood to the Cliff Edge fence, opens the gate, and plants herself in a defensive posture along the Cliff Edge awaiting the appearance of her rival. Holding pressure on her self induced laceration, she trusts that it will not take long for the Monster to pick up the scent of her Blood, and be at her chosen place for their confrontation. While waiting has a thought about the thing she had seen, and communed with in her strange dream, some days ago.

I'll probably never know who that was supposed be, and why they tried to warn me about someone wanting me to fail.

Then another thought on a positive note crosses her mind, *This plan of mine is going, just the way I designed it!*

Chapter Thirty-Five

RACHAEL DRESSED ALL in black crouches quietly along the edge of the Cliff leaning against the fence, holding her arm, to stop the bleeding, where she waits patiently for her Nemesis. With her full Vampire attributes revealed; including of course, her heightened hearing, and night vision, and the strength of many, she stays very still and listens for its approach; thankfully she's glad that the ocean is rather calm tonight making it easier for her to be able to hear it draw near so as to be caught in her trap. Finally, after a few moments, she hears something moving on the other side of the fence making its way to the open gate.

As she watches the open gateway as the head of this monster begins to emerge, luckily it looks first in the opposite direction from where Rachael is waiting for it.

When it turns its head in her direction, showing its red eyes, it opens its mouth to let out a somewhat loud hiss. She now realizes that it can also see in the dark. Hisses back at it, Rachael rises up to her full height of five feet three, seeing her do this it also rises on its hind legs and surprisingly is just a few inches shorter than her. As they begin to move slowly closer to each other, Rachael has a quick questioning thought,

How does a Raccoon get to be so tall? But this is certainly no ordinary Raccoon, now is it?

As it gets close enough to lunge at her, she opens two of her fingers of her hand, from the still oozing self inflicted wound on her arm and the pressure of her Blood sprays into the Coons face, blinding it just long enough for her to take hold of its head in her hands, so as to twist it to the side for her to be able to bite into it's neck, but before she can accomplish this, it lashes out blindly and catches her shoulder to sink its claws in deep, tearing her blouse sleeve from her shoulder. She winces in pain, but makes no sound, as she swiftly moves her right hand to the area under its left arm to clear the way to its neck, to be able to sink her teeth in hard, in only seconds she has sucked out enough of its Blood for it to eventually go limp in her hands. All during their entanglement her wound also sprays her Blood on the fence, and the ground and down the Cliff side spattering the rocks all the way down to the water.

As this Monster Raccoon finally goes limp in her hands, she lays it down on the ground, tears off what's left of her Bloody sleeve and drops it down the Cliff, tearing off the other sleeve to wrap her arm wound, also tearing off some of the front of her blouse to hold over her shoulder wound. Then, with her foot, pushes the now lifeless carcass of her adversary over the Cliff Edge along with one of her shoes. Her other shoe she just leaves there on the ground. Slowly, painfully and warily, she makes her way down the Cliff onto the shoreline, and then walks along it to a place where she can get back up to the vacant lot, and back to the house. In the Kitchen, she removes a bottle of Wine from the Fridge, takes a long, deep swallow, and then puts it back in the Refrigerator. She makes her way carefully, not letting any of her Blood drip to the floor on the way to the second floor Bathroom, to clean her wounds and freshen up, then to her Bedroom to change her clothes, readying herself for her well planned nocturnal get away. Luckily, her wounds have now stopped bleeding. After dressing herself, fixing her makeup, applying the blond wig, putting the clothing from the conflict in a bag to take with her and dispose of somewhere far from here, feeling ready to go now.

She slowly walks down the Grand Staircase for what she strongly feels will be her last time; turning round at the bottom and says,

"Goodbye ol' House, and Goodbye, Marlena!"

Giving a moment for a reply from Marlena, but not from the house, of course.

At about the same time up in the Attic, Marlena sees a bright light growing larger and coming closer in front of her. At first she's not too sure what it is, thinking it could just be the full moon shining through the window, until the middle of it reveals to her the ethereal images of her Daughter Gabrielle and her Husband James beckoning her to walk through, she hesitates at first having a small amount of resistance, but finally gives in, and enters the light, and as she does the ethereal image of her Son Jimmy comes into view, and for some strange reason she receives the knowledge that her Son was a victim of Rachael's Blood Passion. With this enlightenment she turns to make the attempt to go back through to the Attic, but an unseen barrier bars her way, so turns back to her Son Jimmy, and embraces him.

Rachael sits in her Car in the garage slightly puzzled why Marlena did not say Goodbye to her. Takes in a deep breath and presses the button to open the door slowly and as quietly as possible drives away down Cedar Lane, not turning on the headlights until reaching where it connects to Cedar Road.

Heads for Route Ninety Five which will take her through Connecticut and eventually to the state of New York, where she plans to dump the Car off the side of the road, make her way to a nearby town acquire a Vehicle to return to the place of the staged crash to retrieve her belongings.

After driving Route Ninety Five all most till overcast daylight she gets near to the border of Connecticut and New York State just outside of the town of Stamford, finding a dark secluded place on the highway, she takes a corner short and goes off the road side swiping a tree, obtaining no injury to herself, she goes under the dash to give the impression that someone hot wired the Car, smashes the driver side window, cleans up most of the glass so it doesn't look like it happened at the scene of the accident, although it could have.

Before leaving to go into town to make use of her new identity, covering the Car with some fallen tree branches to hide it, after acquiring another Vehicle and going back to her Car, transfers all her stuff to the new Car and heads north to a little, but famous town along the Hudson River in upper New York State called Sleepy Hollow, where she has prearranged plans on staying at a quaint little Bed and Breakfast for awhile.

Very early in the morning following the night that Rachael had made her getaway from the Cliff House. Her Mother, Mina shows up unannounced for a visit, finding the place strangely empty, but some of the lights are still on so using her key goes in to have a look around. Searching the house, it seems to her that all Rachael's things are still there, Mina gets a strong weird feeling that something is amiss, goes out back and is stunned to see Blood on the Backyard Porch steps, she follows it to the Gate in the Fence, finding the Gate open, continuing with her search only to see that there are signs that a struggle had taken place. She is quite stunned, when she sees a large amount of Blood on the fence and also a Blood trail leading over and down the Cliff. She then notices a Woman's shoe with Blood stains on it, back in the house, sitting in the Living Room holding the shoe, Mina sorrowfully thinks,

Rachael, my Dear sweet Child, what could have happened here?

As it gets a little brighter outside, she hears a number of Cars pull up on the street in front of the Cliff House; she goes out front to find two Police Cars parked on the street. She approaches, what appears to be the Officer in charge, inquiring,

"Excuse me Officer, but why are you here?"

"There's no call for alarm, Miss… Mrs.…ah?"

"That's Mrs.… Mrs. DeClerico, Mrs. Mina DeClerico!"

The Officer continues as he points to the empty lot,

"We're here to remove the caution tape from the vacant lot over there, and make sure that there's no problem here!"

"Well, if it's all the same to you Officer…ah? There is a problem here, well not out here per say, but out back of my Daughter's house."

"I'm Sergeant Walker, Sergeant Al Walker,"

He points at Thirty Cedar Lane and continues,

"Do you mean this house, the Cliff House?"

"I most certainly do!"

"Did you say out back?"

"Yes, I did!"

"I think maybe we'd better have a look out there? But first please do tell me a little of what it is that you'd found."

Mina hands the shoe to him and tells of what she had seen on the Cliff side of the fence, the Police make their way to the Backyard and do a preliminary investigation; their findings are that there was a struggle along the Cliff Edge and both assailants probably fell to their death. They return to Mina, waiting out front by her Car to inform her of their findings. She is shocked, and begins to sop, asking,

"Are you telling me my Daughter might be dead?"

"We're not sure just who might have died, if anyone, it will take more investigating to determine that. When was the last time you had contact with your Daughter?"

"About four days ago!"

"Well, we'll have a C.S.I. team from New London out here as soon as possible to have a look."

"Thank you Officer Walker, here is my contact numbers and address, please if you find anything, or need me for anything just contact me. I really need to go now, please."

"Of course, Mrs. DeClerico, you're free to go!"

As Mina drives away from the Cliff House saying aloud,

"That **damn** house! First Michael, now my Rachael!"

Epilogue

RACHAEL PULLS INTO the parking lot of the Riverside Bed and Breakfast in the town of Sleepy Hollow, New York State located on the banks of the Hudson River, and parks. Exits it with only her small overnight bag for now. Before ascending the five steps to the entrance door she, turns round to view the flowing water of the River just across the road.

The gentle sinuousness of the water gives her the feeling of calmness. Turning back to the stairs, she begins to ascend them, when suddenly the side entry door bursts open, slightly startled she grips the handle of her case in her right hand and the banister in her left tightly, moving to the side giving room for them to get by her, as two young children swiftly run down the stairs and over by a Car in the lot, immediately following them two adults come out telling the children not to be in such a rush. Rachael has a silent giggle, remembering what it was like to be a child, and excited about something.

Taking just a moment, to compose herself, before proceeding up the stairs, once at the door, opens it and walks in, is then greeted warmly by a very handsome older Man with white hair standing behind a counter pronouncing,

"Welcome young Miss," As he holds out his hand to provide her with a pen, continuing with, "I would imagine you do have a reservation with us, so if you would be so kind, as to sign the register, please?"

Then, as this kindly old gentleman gestures to the young man seated in a chair to their right, he continues with, "Then I'll have young Benjamin here; show you to your room."

Rachael takes the pen from him answering,

"Yes, I do Sir, thank you."

"Sir, is not necessary, you can address me by my name."

"I certainly would, if I knew it!"

"It's Michael, but most folks round here just call me, Mike!"

She then lowers her head to look down at the registration ledger, as her eyes widen, and a wry smile appears on her face, putting the pen to the page, entering her name into the registry.

'Mia Harkness'

BONUS NOVELLA

BLOOD PASSION

~Prequel~

Inception

J.M. VALENTE

NOTE TO READER;

I sincerely apologize to you, and all my readers; that I am not able to divulge, how I came about obtaining the information that made it possible to write this **Blood Passion** prequel Novella. But, please do, enjoy and be satisfied with obtaining the extraordinary account of how and why, this intriguing and eclectic story, of which I have come to designate as my, **Blood Passion Saga,** began and has come to be written.

J. M. Valente

Contents

CHAPTER ONE

DEEP IN THE jungle, on what is recognized as the Continent of Central America on the Planet, Earth; in the Milky Way Galaxy, which is known and named by the Human Being inhabitants; as the country of Mexico. A good distance outside of its Capital metropolis: Mexico City, under the cover of darkness, and silent as the grave, a large weird looking Alien spherical craft, evidently from a Planet outside of our universe, once more came to a stealthily landing in a small clearing. I was not awakened by its landing.

In the morning, when I awoke at my small camp site not far from their landing place to observe unseen, and undetected by these extraterrestrial beings, in all my travels, I have 'ant encountered anything like it, or them before. Which are beyond description of this, or just about any other worlds' understanding, it seemed to me from what I could make out that they were on, some type of peaceful mission to populate the uninhabited Planets of any, and all the Solar Systems that they have, or will encounter in their vast interstellar travels. I can't say how, but at this time, I comprehended this, just a very strong, strange feeling in my acute common sense. Keeping out of sight, I watched as these beings grouped, outside their ship. What seemed to me to be the foremost scientist of them gives orders by mental telepathy, I could sense, because being close enough to hear any sounds they might make, I could hear nothing, but the crew members nodded and gestured in recognition, of something being communicated to them, and to go about their business, whom it seems, are trained in seeking out the location of certain animal species that have ingested the DNA of the most highly mentally evolved indigenous creatures of this Planet. For which they have, for a long time, come to be known as Homo-Sapiens.

My understanding of this is only my best educated guess of what they are up to, but in the end my cultured guessing turns out to be correct, because for some strange reason, what they are conveying mentally I begin to be able to hear in my mind, and understand their intentions. Some kind of advanced Alien interpreting, I would think.

May I say, that it's quite fascinating, because even though their language is still incoherent to me, I can comprehend what they mean, I now understand, that too many times before have they failed to succeed in this endeavor, at the orders of their superiors; they must find a way to fulfill their assignment. Their failures thus far have created some of the most hideous of creatures, only some of them have lived a very short time, because they had to be destroyed. The temporary abductions, of numerous living beings from the Planets they have visited, have supplied them with large amounts of Blood, and DNA samples, with their advanced knowledge of, what we would distinguish as cloning; they have the highly developed technologies to create living animated creatures in their Ship's Laboratories. Because, thus far they have failed, to create a living being that is superior to anything on our Planet or any Planet outside of their own.

They will, and must continue with their mission; that is to seek out the missing elements, so as to succeed, and plant the seed of life elsewhere that will thrive better than this one has, or ever will.

As I've come to understand it and foretold you, their supply of DNA comes from many other worlds throughout our and numerous other solar systems, for they have traveled far and wide in their pursuit of creating a better being than any that they have created before, and have seeded many worlds with, including our own.

Their dilemma has been coming across the right combination of DNA to do this successfully. They shall not cease, until they have succeeded in creating an almost perfect living being, even better than themselves, for they do consider themselves to be the most highly evolved, and advanced species in the known inhabited, and yet to be inhabited worlds, that they have seeded, or will seed and visited in their travels, by our worlds' measurement of time that would be roughly five hundred million years.

Their science teams using their locator instruments, somewhat like our GPS devices go about finding the locations of the supposed Blood, and DNA they may need to appropriate. The top members among them once again meet to consider what to try, or better yet, what they haven't tried, they converse and finally realize, that they need more than a combination of only two DNA, which is what they believed was the only way to accomplish their task, but now they need to consider perhaps adding a third or more to the mix, which is something, to the best of their knowledge, that they, or their predecessors have not considered doing, and they wonder why not.

As they go back inside their vessel, I find my way inside their craft through what seemed to me as a Ventilator Air Duct with a damaged grate; I keep myself hidden, to watch and take in what they are communicating to one another.

One of them activates, on a handheld Computer type mechanism, a holographic video image showing the past documented trials of this type, to discover that there has been no success, thus far, in using more than two DNA types, as a matter of fact, any trials turned out worse than just using a combination of two DNA, none of the test subjects ever lived for any length of time, they now assume that the combinations in these past trials, were not sufficient enough to bring success. They then began to go over the combinations of the types of DNA that was used in these prior tests, after long considerations, they start to realize the error in all of these past trials; of a three or more DNA amalgamation of all the test subjects' the Blood must be of precise, accurate amounts, when incorporated together, so the Blood must be blended to extremely perfect measurements first, before infusing it into a host or unborn embryo. With these somewhat, for them, simple findings, they realize that, what must be missing is that although infusing their own DNA, with that of the existing Human being inhabitance of a world, which has worked numerous times, although the results have been very successful, but with no clear advancement, beyond what results they have been getting in mental or physical abilities of their creations, in other Solar Systems on other Planets, the result has been somewhat the same every time, on all the Planets they have attempted it.

Their explicit instructions are to find the way to create a more advanced species of Humanoid by any means possible. They now realize that they only have one of the Blood samples that they need, to accomplish their mission. They will at lease need two others, so they inform the science team of their new task and give them their new instructions on getting them what they now need, and the equipment to do so, while they begin to set up for these new experiments.

CHAPTER TWO

THESE ALIEN BEINGS, who have finally come to realize after close rigorous study of the past procedures, of only infusing the DNA of their own race and a Humanoid being of a Planet's inhabitants, is not enough to make the advancements they are trying for. They have now and finally realized that they must mix the DNA of a third subject into the procedure in order to even come close to any success.

They have now come to the understanding that the unambiguous third subject must be a species of the Planet's animal life, which feeds off the Planets Humanoid beings Blood, so that they have ingested Humanoid DNA on a regular basis. It must be a multi mixture of Blood from all of the subjects involved, which will now include; one of their own kind, one of this Planets Humanoid beings, and the missing key, for any kind of success, an animal type species known to this Planet as Vampire Bats. So while they will await the field team's return, they begin to make ready their underground Laboratory for these new trials, then using this Blood combination serum, as a catalyst.

Then infusing it into an impregnated Female of the chosen animal species of the Vampire Bat, because past procedures have taught them that an animal has a greater chance of success and they will get quicker results. Also, because animals have natural multi full births, giving them a better chance that one or more of the newborn will be advanced and survive. If they are successful with the animal, they would then try using a Female Human subject of our world.

The field team now ready with their advanced mechanisms for locating and acquiring what is needed, they go out to accomplish their task, which will hopefully and eventually create a better Humanoid race than their predecessors have done on this Planet or any Planet in the past, the team is given their orders of what is needed; first and foremost is to abduct a young adult Male Human being, for this new trial experiment. The team takes their leave of the ship, to the rural area outside of the city so as to do this unseen or undetected by anyone.

Their – as we on earth would describe them – Medical Team makes the final preparations in the Lab, as I have aforementioned, they have now decided to use three specific types of Blood; the Blood for this trial must be fresh, the Blood supplies that they keep in storage will not do.

The field team returns with; a large Male and Female Vampire Bat, also an unconscious young adult Male Humanoid, which immediately is brought into the Laboratory for the extraction of several vials of his Blood, he then will be returned from whence he came with no knowledge of this encounter or ordeal. Now with all they need; they can begin to create the combined serum to be injected into the large artificially impregnated Female Vampire Bat that they have now in captivity. First, they will extract an unfertilized egg from this same Vampire Bat, for a backup cloning trial. After they do the initializing of both experiments, they will have to wait in our Planet's time for the proper incubation periods, so in the interim, they will leave their lab team to monitor the proceedings in the hidden, underground Laboratory they built beneath an ancient Mayan monument, many of our Planet's years ago. The ship will then go about their clandestine business of their other many information gathering operations, they have here on Earth, what they refer to as Planet three six five.

Once the Laboratory team has any results successful or not, by their means of communications, they will then contact their craft, and then the ship will return for the latest findings of the experiments.

It only took me a moment to find and make my way through the Ventilation, Air Shaft, to the underground Laboratory, so I believed I had not missed anything vital, where I could continue to observe and listen.

Now, considering my own wellbeing, I find that I'm somewhat low of my supplies, and realizing it's going to be some time before any results are known, I took this opportunity to leave my hiding place to return to the small town that I was staying in, to replenish my food and water supply, get cleaned up in the small hotel where I had a room. And once these tasks are accomplished, I would make my way back, to hopefully witness the results of their experiments.

CHAPTER THREE

AS I MADE my way back to my hiding place with my restocked previsions, I had some very strange images in my mind, of an Alien Planets' life, most likely the effect of being able to understand them and acquiring some of their memories, what I had visions of, in my mind, were truly fascinating, and totally indescribable in our Planets' English language.

Now back in my hiding place I once again watched and listened, but observed no major results had happened while I was absent. So I settled in for some much needed rest, for the journey to town and back was long, treacherous and tiring.

I was startled awake, by a commotion in the Laboratory, I heard in my mind what seemed like the Lab Technicians were elated with some of the results of the cloning of the Vampire Bat embryo. Of what I could see, it looked like it has matured over night, they were communicating, but more like debating, on the finding that it was about three months old; one began to accuse another of tampering with the experiment, by infusing an Alien substance they had found on a B-Class Planet in a quadrant they had named six six six of the Betjing Galaxy. The head Tec stormed into the Lab to adamantly proclaim that he had done this thing, to hopefully achieve the results they have been trying to obtain for far too long. So now with things looking successful for them it was time for me to make another trip back to town, to hopefully obtain some items I had been waiting to arrive from my own Lab in Hartford, Connecticut, to be able to record and continue my surveillance of these Aliens' operations, for I will certainly want to have proof of all this.

The next day, on my way back to my hiding place in the underground Laboratory Ventilation, Air Shaft, unfortunately without my sent for equipment, for they had not arrived as of yet, I ran into a native of the land, frantically running for his life toward me, spouting something in his native language that I could not make out, although it somewhat sounded like the Mayan dialect to me, what I could see was that he was truly frightened by something that he saw or heard.

Continuing on with my return trip, I came upon a clearing in the jungle, to be confronted by a strange creature, that I had never seen before in my life, it appeared to be like a Bat, but it was very altered, it had to be the Mutated Vampire Bat that was created by the Aliens, it's alterations, as I could observe were as such; rather large in size, it was bigger than any bat I've ever seen before, it had longer fangs than any Bat I have ever observed, and its face... oh my Lord, it's face looked almost Human. At the same moment I took notice of, and heard in my mind, the Alien hunters coming from behind this creature, communicating something about capturing the escaped artificially created animal to bring it back to the Lab to be transported to another Planet to populate it. I swiftly hid myself into some nearby thick foliage and watched, as they tried to capture the strange animal with their devices, but they didn't have much luck, for it took flight inelegantly to gradually disappear over the horizon in the direction of Mexico City.

I waited, for the time it took for the Aliens to leave the clearing, only then did I make my way out of my hiding place to see their spherical Spaceship lift off, and disappear out of the Earth's Atmosphere, I then went to the location of the underground Laboratory Ventilation Air Shaft, only to find it had been sealed up with rocks, and dirt, that appeared to be melted into a solid barrier, the ground near by revealing to my observing eyes many frantic footprints of the Aliens', and what almost certainly were the Mutated Vampire Bats' prints leading off into the jungle. Of course, there were no signs that any craft had landed, they had just about covered up any signs of evidence of the event except for the footprints, but the wind and the rain would get rid of those soon enough, and me like an idiot with no camera to record them. I had missed my once in a lifetime chance to get undisputed evidence of all these strange occurrences of the past few days.

I had often told myself, to always carry a camera of some sort with me, but like an absent minded fool, I had failed to listen and exercise my own advice. I had sent to my Lab in Hartford for my video equipment, but alas, it had not arrived in time.

Chiding myself,

"You idiot!"

I then resigned myself, to the fact that discovering what happened, to lead to this creatures' escaping from the alien Laboratory, would evidently not be ever known to me. Sadly, this was the end of **my** extraordinary adventure, but I would surmise would be the inception of another for **someone else**.

A beginning.

Continued in **BLOOD PASSION,** *the first Novel of*

J.M. Valente's Modern Gothic American Horror Saga.

Available in print at On-Line Booksellers,

Or Order from your Local Bookstore,

Also available in e-Book editions.

CPSIA information can be obtained
at www.ICGtesting.com
Printed in the USA
BVHW031154180719
553829BV00005B/112/P

9 781643 989648